CLIMBING KILIMANJARO

Sequel to THE BOYZIE TRILOGY

John Broome

All characters and most of the places in this novel are entirely fictitious.
No reference to anyone alive or dead is intended.

Trafford
PUBLISHING

Order this book online at www.trafford.com/08-0609
or email orders@trafford.com

Most Trafford titles are also available at major online book retailers.

Edited by: Jill Todd

Note for Librarians: A cataloguing record for this book is available from Library
and Archives Canada at www.collectionscanada.ca/amicus/index-e.html

Printed in Victoria, BC, Canada.

ISBN: 978-1-4251-7821-5

*We at Trafford believe that it is the responsibility of us all, as both individuals
and corporations, to make choices that are environmentally and socially sound.
You, in turn, are supporting this responsible conduct each time you purchase a
Trafford book, or make use of our publishing services. To find out how you are
helping, please visit www.trafford.com/responsiblepublishing.html*

*Our mission is to efficiently provide the world's finest, most comprehensive
book publishing service, enabling every author to experience success.
To find out how to publish your book, your way, and have it available
worldwide, visit us online at www.trafford.com/10510*

Trafford
PUBLISHING™

www.trafford.com

North America & international
toll-free: 1 888 232 4444 (USA & Canada)
phone: 250 383 6864 ♦ fax: 250 383 6804
email: info@trafford.com

The United Kingdom & Europe
phone: +44 (0)1865 722 113 ♦ local rate: 0845 230 9601
facsimile: +44 (0)1865 722 868 ♦ email: info.uk@trafford.com

10 9 8 7 6 5 4 3 2 1

For:

The Lady Olivia, and the four "Guides" who preceeded her:

Wanda, Star, Faith and Fergie.

My Faithful companions, good friends and true, who "walked beside me" over the past 30 years!

John Broome
Author

Thanks are due to the following persons for their help, loyalty, devotion and friendship during the preparation of this publication:

To Tim at Trafford Publishing (U.K.) for all his help and his sense of sense of humour.

To Jill Todd, my Editor, for all her guidance and good advice.

To Kate and Bryan Southwood for all the help they so kindly gave me, and for their friendship.

For all the staff and inmates who work in the Braille Unit at HMP Full Sutton.

Without them, I would not have been able to read the transcripts prior to my sending them off for publication. Thank you!

For Dave, who called me "Dad" – a friend indeed.

You bucked me up so many times when I was feeling down.

Thanks "Son".

And finally, to my Bunny – my best friend in the whole world (bar none).

She knows what for!

John Broome

1

IT WAS a fine, although rather chilly, morning at the beginning of March 1990, the first Monday in March and just after 10 a.m. I had eaten a hearty breakfast, showered, shaved and now I was up and dressed, sitting in the television room situated across from the ward in which I currently occupied a bed at the County Hospital in Gaynsford, North Midlands.

Nurse Helen Tidy had just come into the room.

"Oh, there you are, Boyzie! They are all waiting for you back in the ward!"

"What? Who?"

"Sister Brennan and the doctors, and Andy!"

"Oh well, I'd better put in an appearance then, eh nurse?"

Arm in arm with Nurse Helen Tidy, a tall and not unattractive blonde, who had been very kind to me during my enforced sojourn at the County Hospital, I walked back to the four-bedded ward that I shared with three other guys. A reception committee was awaiting my arrival! Doctor Mishra was there. She was a young Asian woman with a keen sense of humour, and she and I had always got along very well together, ever since my admission and her first involvement with me. Doctor Chen was there, also Mr Newbold, the surgeon who undertook the operation that virtually saved my life!

My new mate, Andrew David Gange, a young ex-police constable, who had lost practically all the sight in one eye due to acid having been thrown into his face while he was on duty in the town centre, was also present at the meeting. Andy and I had become firm friends, especially since the decease of the late Paul McGowan, who had recently shared the ward with us and a guy called Scott Jacklin, who was in the hospital because he had sustained injuries following a motorcycle accident. The four of us had been great mates, and the shock of Paul's death had affected all of us, including the staff who worked on our wing.

Andy had asked me to move in with him. He had a flat in a large, end-of-terrace house in the town centre, but recently we had discussed the idea of Andy coming to live with me in Milling Street, Osleston. The purpose of the meeting was to continue the discussion and hopefully come to some definite conclusions prior to both of us being discharged from the hospital to my new home - the council house I had acquired on my return to Gaynsford from Harts Hill - 30 Milling Street, Osleston, the coming weekend.

I was glad that Andy had decided to move into my home and share with me! Being blind, I was used to my own home environment. I would feel much more comfortable living there than I would have done if I had moved once more to Depot Street where Andy had previously lived prior to his admission to the hospital. In the company of two social workers, and Nurse Jenny Baxter from the hospital, Andy and I had been to look around his flat together, and although it was large, and, I believed, could have been made very comfortable with a deal of 'tender loving care', which had not been lavished upon it hitherto, I was not really sold on the idea of moving in with Andy and living there permanently. Yes! I was sure the best solution was Andy moving to Milling Street with me, and Andy himself seemed very happy with his choice.

I had written, or rather my brother, Eric, had written, to the borough council, asking if I could have permission to have a lodger with me in the house, and explaining my circumstances. The council had sent a young woman to the hospital to talk to Andy and me, and following Mary Randle's visit it was agreed that, under the circumstances, I could have Andy to live with me. He would undertake the role of my carer, a role for which he would receive an allowance - a carer's allowance that would be paid monthly into his bank account.

He had the offer of a job with the police at the Bread Street Divisional Headquarters, working in the community support team in an administrative capacity, so he would be staying 'on the Force'. As for me! Well, I would look for work once I felt completely restored to full health, and until then I would draw incapacity benefit and receive other help, i.e. with the rent for the house, some kind of daily living allowance etc., etc.

I would require a cleaner when I got home, but Andy reckoned his family, he had eight sisters, would sort all that out among themselves, and we would have no worries on that score! Good! It was one less headache for me, and heaven knew, I would have enough of them without concerning myself with domestic issues! We were both extremely positive. Both of us yearned to get out into the world once more, so we portrayed ourselves as being ready; ready to face whatever might occur, ready to help one another, ready to work together for our mutual benefit!

The four members of the hospital staff who were present at the meeting that day listened intently and eventually agreed that we should both be discharged home to 30 Milling Street, Heath Road Estate, Osleston, Gaynsford, on Saturday, 10th March 1990.

2

Boyzie - summary of past events.

ON 3RD May 1978, my late wife, Susan, had been admitted to the County Hospital, and on the following day she was transferred to the Mary Craigie Unit at the College Hospital, where she subsequently died on Monday 8th May, just two days after our gracious team, Gaynsford United, had won the FA League Challenge Cup. I had been down at the home ground in Gaynsford, North Midlands, on that glorious afternoon, watching the FA League Challenge Cup Final, which was being played down at Wembley Stadium, and was also being relayed to us at our home stadium, packed to capacity, on about 20 wide screens situated around the ground. It was an American idea, an experiment on that wonderful and never-to-be-forgotten day! It was an experiment that worked extremely well, which later on was used to great effect both nationally and internationally for all kinds of situations, including relaying sport to the masses. We were part of the pilot scheme back then in 1978 - but I digress!

I had greatly enjoyed that experience, together with loads and loads of my mates and acquaintances, but had always felt guilty that I had been there instead of spending time with my late and still lamented wife, whom I adored and revered. She had told me to go and enjoy myself, so I had! We had arranged that I would spend the following day, Sunday, with her and she had booked me into the unit for lunch.

"I'm told they cook a smashing Sunday roast here," she said. I had very much looked forward to spending the time with her on that pleasantly warm May day - the day after our glorious win, after all, I had so much to tell her. When I arrived at the Mary Craigie Unit that morning, Nurse Lesley Helen Peters, who was well known to me, told me Susan was very poorly. On the following day, Monday, 8th May 1978, my lovely Susan had passed away quietly in her slumber, never to hear all the things I had wished to tell her - or the love words I still had to say to her. She knew how much I loved her, oh yes, my darling, you knew, didn't you? How could you not? Our love was so great, so very, very wonderful and great.

After she died I went to stay with her brother, Mick, and his family. I slept for the first couple of nights beside her brother, who looked after me and was a source of great comfort to me, as I believe I was to him. We consoled one another in our time of mutual sorrow, and by so doing we became very close, like brothers.

On Tuesday, 16th May at 10.45 a.m., her funeral took place at the same church where we were married in August 1966, and the same vicar, the Reverend John Lammie, officiated. He said some lovely things about my late wife. A great number of my relations were present at Susan's funeral, 14 of them in fact, including my parents, a family friend, Eleanor Newman, my aunts and uncles on my mother's side of the family, plus my brother and his wife, and also my sister, Doreen, and her husband, Fred, whom I had not expected to be present. Everyone made me promise that as soon as I felt able to do so, I would go and visit them wherever they lived in the country.

§≈∾§

On Saturday, 12th August 1978, I set off on a month's holiday to undertake the promises I had made to all my relatives at the time of my late wife's funeral. I kept remembering the last words Susan had said to me before she died.

"Don't cry! I'm comfortable! I'm happy. Please be happy for me,

Boyzie!"

She had then sighed, turned her face from me and gone to sleep, and she never spoke again. I also remembered how she had joshed with me and told me that she hoped I would marry again once she was dead! Of course, I had been very guarded about my answer to the question.

"Boyzie? When I have gone, will you marry again?"

"No! I don't think so!" I said, eventually.

She had almost shouted.

"Oh, you mustn't say that! You ought to marry again. I won't be here, and you need someone to care for you! Promise me you will marry again when the time is right, and if you meet someone you love! Promise?"

"No!" I said, and indeed, she never did elicit that promise from me!

As I say, on 12th August 1978 I travelled down to stay with my parents in Thamesford, Essex, and then we went to Seaport in West Sussex to the wedding of my cousin, Queenie, who was the eldest daughter of my Aunt Nelly and Uncle Alf Sunley. I stayed with them for a week then returned to Essex before I went off to spend a long weekend with my brother, Eric, and his family in Cherry Wootton, down in East Anglia. It was while I was staying with Eric and his wife, Yvonne, that I met and fell madly in love with Johnquel Amelia Friscoe - Johnnie Friscoe!

Seductive, warm, friendly, sociable, funny, glamorous, glorious, with a keen sense of fun! She loved driving, loved me and I loved her! I loved her with a passion - an intense and overwhelming passion that threatened to engulf me. I wanted her! I wanted to be with her, to please her, to take her! 'Come into my parlour', said the spider to the fly! Yes, and how easily and willingly this 'fly' acquiesced! Johnquel Amelia Friscoe! Joyful, loving, adored and revered by me - Johnnie Friscoe - sly, cunning, stealthy, wheedling and ferocious in her lovemaking. Johnnie Friscoe the psychopath! She had spun a web that totally ensnared me, albeit I was not an unwilling participant in her entrapment! I was completely bowled over by her.

My brother, Eric, and his wife, Eve, endeavoured to warn me of her somewhat erratic and, at times, bizarre behaviour, but when one is in love, one does not listen to the voice of reason. Thus, I made great play of telling them both that I was sure everything would be fine, and that I wanted to see her again. ·

On the Sunday, just prior to my leaving Cherry Wootton to travel up to stay with my sister, Doreen, and her family, I said my fond farewell to Johnnie by telephone, saying that I hoped we would meet again very soon. At that time I had no notion of how soon that meeting might be scheduled to take place. In the event, we did not see one another on that occasion, but she saw me in the company of another woman, Sandy Christmas! I had met her and her family whilst travelling up to Harts Hill on that Sunday afternoon towards the end of August 1978. Sandy and I had talked for most of our journey northwards and, on arrival in the town of Brigthorpe, she had made me promise that I would visit her and her cousin, Norma, and that maybe we would all go out somewhere on the following Sunday, maybe to Donkey Meadow. I willingly and happily made such a promise to the very amusing, friendly and warm-hearted woman. Yes, I wanted to see Sandy Christmas again! Her four young offspring were quite delightful. During our journey northwards, we had chatted gaily and hardly stopped laughing!

On the appointed day for our next meeting and the subsequent outing to Donkey Meadow, the August weather could not have been better if it had been made to order! We took a huge picnic with us, and there were a lot of people present for the family outing. Sandy and I had a great time, at least initially. We found the shelter of some shady trees and settled ourselves, minus the four youngsters, who had engaged in play with other children of the family, and enjoyed a sumptuous repast. Afterwards, we stretched out while the kids continued to play.

We lay together beneath the welcome canopy of the trees on Donkey Meadow. We believed we were safe from prying eyes, so we indulged ourselves! We made passionate love together beneath those shady trees on that wonderful August afternoon, but as we did so, I had no idea of the consequences that would ensue!

Johnnie had driven up from her home in the south in an effort to surprise me, but she was the one to get a surprise! Seeing me making love to another woman, a black woman at that, for Sandy was of mixed race, was all too much for Johnnie, and it tipped her over the edge of sanity, albeit temporarily. In her rage she left the woods and Donkey Meadow to return home to Berkshire unfulfilled.

On the fringes of the moor she met up with four lost little boys, who were engaged in play. Two of them were the sons of Sandy Christmas, two the twin sons of Sandy's cousin, Babs. Johnnie spoke to them, enquiring if they knew the location of Donkey Meadow, and they replied in the affirmative, offering to show the 'nice lady' the way! Johnnie had already been there once that afternoon, but she still went along with the four little boys, and as she walked she asked them where they were from. Randall and Dominic, the two sons of Sandy Christmas, told her they were staying in Harts Hill, and she asked them if they knew a bloke called Boyzie. Randall, who had become great pals with me, immediately said:

"Oh, yeh! He's a friend of our mam and he's here with us today, lady!"

Johnnie already knew that, of course! The spider's web had been spun and, with a little help, she had managed to ensnare the fly! She then suggested that perhaps she did not need to see me after all, and asked the older boys if they would like ice creams, chocolate, lemonade etc., to which they naturally replied:

"Ooh, yes please, kind lady!"

They were just kids. They thought the lady was good and kind! Oh God, if they had only known the hatred that was seething within her heart for me at that moment. Entirely oblivious to that, they allowed her to take them off with her and buy them the desired ice creams, chocolate, crisps, toffees and soft drinks. They walked, they talked, they ran and played silly games together, and the 'kind lady' participated in all the fun happily and willingly! In the late evening, she led them back to the path where she had met them, sending them on their way with kisses and hugs, and even some cash in their pockets. Oh, she had done her work well, had Johnnie Friscoe!

The lads loved her and wanted to protect her from harm when the family members questioned them about what had been happening and where they had been during the five hours or so that they had been away. I asked them lots of questions, and Randall and Dominic did their best to answer truthfully, although they were scared of getting the 'nice lady' into trouble. They were more scared of their mam, who seemed very angry that they had been away enjoying themselves, although everyone else seemed to have been doing the same; playing games, eating from the picnic baskets, lying in the sunshine or in the shade, drinking, generally having a great time! Randall reasoned through his tears, why shouldn't they have done the same? Of course, he and his younger brother, plus the twins, who were only tots, were all far too young to realise the consequences of what had occurred during that very long, hot sultry afternoon! They only knew they had thoroughly enjoyed themselves with the very kind lady, and the other grownups seemed to resent it.

I was the real sufferer in all this! To assuage my own fears and because of the safety of my own family in Harts Hill, my sister, Doreen, had 13 children, I cut short my holiday with Doreen and Fred Dingle and returned home to Gaynsford a few days earlier than I had intended. I had believed that was the end of the saga, but it wasn't, in fact, it was only the first scene in the drama!

§❧§

I had been talking to my brother, Eric, and his wife, Eve, who paid a surprise visit to the hospital on Thursday, during the late afternoon. At first all three of us and my mate, Andy Gange, walked together in the grounds and sat under some trees on a bench seat at the end of the beautifully kept gardens that surrounded the County Hospital. We had been discussing the coming weekend and the forthcoming move of myself and Andy back home to the new house, which I had acquired on my return to Gaynsford from Harts Hill. Eric casually said to Andy:

"I bet you would rather be going back to your place, wouldn't you?"

Andy had replied quickly, but jovially, nonetheless.

"No! I'm quite happy to be moving in with Boyzie. We get on great, and I am sure things will stay good between us. I can help him! I'll be able to look after him, and my family will all help. You'll have no worries there, mate, Boyzie will be all right with me, no probs!"

Eric and Eve were still not convinced. Later, when we were alone, just the three of us, Eric pushed £50 into my right hand, and as he shook hands with me on departing he said:

"Look, bruv, it's not really my business, but you *are* my brother, therefore, surely I'm entitled to be concerned about your welfare, yeh?"

"Yeh okay bruv!" I rejoined.

"Then please listen to what I have to say, mate, and then you can make your response! I reckon if you are dead set on this move and want to live with your mate, Andy, then it would be far better if you moved into *his* flat in Depot Street. Why? Because if you do that and it doesn't work out, then if I pay another six months' rent on your place in Milling Street, at least you'll have that to fall back on if things don't work out! If they do, Mike and I will come up and willingly and happily help you to move all your stuff over to Depot Street. How's that sound, bruv?"

I weighed up in my head everything Eric had said, and then quickly replied.

"I don't know what Andy would say! It's all been decided - it's all cut and dried now; the people here know what's happening and Andy's found someone to take over the flat from him, at least, I believe so, anyway."

"Well, perhaps we'd better find out about that then we'll know what's cooking!" said Yvonne, known to all the family as Eve, and Eric concurred.

Eric went off to see if he could find Andy on the pretext of saying goodbye to him, and found him watching television with Bryan Lennon and others in the television lounge across from the ward. To my surprise and relief, Andy came back to the ward with Eric, and we all sat down on my bed and chatted for a while. The upshot of that chat was as follows. Andy and I decided that I would move into his ground floor flat at 10 Depot Street in the town centre opposite the park gates, and Eric would write to the council offering them another six months' rental on the house in Milling Street. There were no bills to pay because I was not inhabiting the property, and Eric had had the telephone disconnected, albeit temporarily. The neighbours were keeping an eye on the place for me, and Yvonne and Eric were going to stay in Gaynsford overnight and then visit my house in Milling Street to see if there was any mail there for me, to give the place a good clean through etc., etc., before they left for home again.

§≈§

On the following Saturday - a warm Saturday in March 1990 - Andy Gange and I left the County Hospital amid many tears and fond farewells from the staff on the wing, to commence life as two good mates living together in the roomy, spacious and well-appointed flat on the ground floor of the three-storey end-of-terrace house at number 10 Depot Street!

It was all very strange and exciting to me, poor deluded fool! I had no concept of what the future held, or of how soon I would begin to regret that move, or even how much I would learn to rue the day I ever met up with Andrew David Gange! For the time being though, all that was some way off, for at that moment all was excitement and joy! The joy of being out of hospital, back in the community again, albeit a strange community - one where I was not 'cock of the walk', as I would undoubtedly have been in my own backyard, so to speak! No! There in the ground floor flat of the house in Depot Street, it was Andy who was 'top dog', and I had to allow him to show me around and, to some extent anyway, was bound to bend to his wishes and desires, and those of his vast family and tribes of mates!

Certainly, life was to be very full of new characters from then on! Certainly too, not all of them were desirable characters, even if most of them were police personnel, but I was to learn all that much later on.

3

IT WAS mid-April 1990, and Harry Devaney was bored! He had been on duty at the Bread Street Police Station for almost 20 hours and had not had much sleep. He was very tired! Nothing much happening, so the morning seemed interminable! Ah well, at 1 p.m. he would be off shift, thank someone up there. He raised his head as he heard a door open, and saw Andy Gange come striding into the small office.

"Hey up, ugly!"

"Watch it, Andy!"

Their playful banter continued for a while, then Andy pushed open the door to the small booth in which Harry Devaney sat and joined him, seating himself opposite him at the table, which was piled high with pamphlets and strewn with forms, envelopes etc.

"You look totally knackered, mate," said Andy.

"You got that right!" exclaimed Harry, rubbing his eyes with his clenched fists. "Roll on 1 p.m. an' I can get aht o' here an' go 'ome to bed for a bit!"

"With whom, Sarge?" asked Andy cheekily.

"Never you mind, laddie," said Devaney, scowling.

Andy chuckled and shuffled his feet beneath the untidy desk.

"How's life then, Andy?" asked DS Harry Devaney, cocking his head on one side.

"Good thanks, Sarge," replied Andy.

He was settling well into the office routine at the police head-quarters, south division, at Bread Street, which was situated almost opposite the Family Support Centre, where Boyzie used to work, and where it was hoped he might recommence work in the near future. For now, his sojourn in the flat in Depot Street, which he shared with Andy, his newfound mate, was working out very well in both their favours.

Andy was essentially lazy and rather indolent. He was slovenly and untidy, although whenever he went on duty, he always looked smart and clean! In his home, however, he was not particularly used to domesticity. Hitherto, his family had endeavoured to keep his flat clean, tidy and habitable. His mother and several of his large family of sisters, he had eight in all, and they all lived close by, would take turns in going around to Depot Street to 'do for' him, but nowadays Andy had his own 'live-in' daily help! Despite his lack of eyesight, Boyzie had proved to be worth his weight in gold, silver and jewels as far as cooking, cleaning, keeping the place tidy etc., went. Andy was delighted, so for him anyway, life was pretty good at present!

"When are you gonna have another of your 'parties'?" asked Harry, with a wicked glint in his eye.

Andy's parties were notorious among the staff at the Bread Street Police Headquarters, many of whom had been present at the functions in the past when all hell was purported to have broken loose!

"Aw! I dunno, Harry. I'd have to ask Boyzie."

"Why? For Chrissake, man, he's only your jockin' lodger, not your keeper!" Harry was saying what a lot of the guys had said to him! "Jimmy Beach and Joe Jackson were asking me only the other day if you were gonna have a house-warming party to welcome you back 'ome like."

Andy smirked.

"Yeh, loads of the lads were askin' me the same thing! Blokes like Martin Connor, Mick Ross and Eddie Blaze. Yeh! Maybe we'll organise something for this weekend, what say, Sarge?"

"Sounds great, and you don't have to ask Boyzie either! He's cum to live wi' yo' an' he'll jus' have to adapt to your ways, eh,

Andy my owd?"

Andy smirked and shuffled his feet beneath the desk.

"Yeh! I reckon you're right, Sarge!" he agreed, and so saying, he stood up and abruptly left the little booth wherein his superior, and a good pal too, was seated, finishing a cuppa before he ended his shift.. Yes! Yes! He'd have a bit of a 'bash' the coming weekend, and Boyzie? Well, he'd just have to put up with it! After all, as Harry had said, he'd moved into Andy's place, and therefore, he must live by Andy's rules from now on! Yeh! It was time he had another 'bash', and he'd invite everyone he could think of! It was time Boyzie met Andy's armies of mates, and time they met him!

Andy had a new spring in his step and a new swagger to his shoulders for the remainder of the day. He was already planning and greatly 'lookin' forrard' to Saturday night and the party at 10 Depot Street, but perhaps he was not looking forward to telling Boyzie about his plans for Saturday night!

.

.

4

Wednesday, 18 April 1990 - 5.45 a.m.

I COULDN'T SLEEP! I was sitting up in bed in the large bed-sitting room on the second floor of Andy's spacious, although rather shabby, flat in Depot Street.

I had made the room comfortable enough, and had fetched plenty of my own belongings and items of my own furniture over to supplement the meagre stock of items that were in there when I first arrived. There were two bunk beds, a large put-you-up sofa, two rather shabby armchairs, two long coffee tables, one containing a large cracked vase, and two chests of drawers, together with a built-in wardrobe and plenty of cupboards. There was also an old fridge, which was free-standing, but which Andy admitted was not staying and suggested that perhaps I either buy a new one or bring mine from Milling Street. In the event, I decided to buy a new one with a small freezer on the top and the big fridge below. I asked him to remove the large put-you-up sofa, the two chairs, the coffee tables and the cracked vase, and the bunk beds.

As I have said, it was a very spacious flat containing four bedrooms, and there was room enough for some of that old furniture to be stored once it was removed from the large bedsit he had allowed me to inhabit. I was happy because I could put my own mark on the room, and Andy even called on one of his mates, a bloke called Bill Ellis, to come around and undertake some decoration of the room for me, as well as paying for a new carpet to be fitted prior to my moving in my own furniture etc. Little did I know that I would pay for his kindness and consideration later! Oh yes, I would! No danger! At that moment in time I considered him to be a good and generous mate, who was anxious that I should feel as comfortable as possible in my new surroundings. How trusting I had become! What a crass idiot, but that was my nature! Despite everything that had happened to me in the recent past, I still trusted people I liked, believing they would never do me any harm. How naive can a person be? Certainly, they didn't come much more naive than me, that's for sure!

I was looking forward to that day, and why wouldn't I be? At 3.15 p.m. I had an interview for a post as a counsellor at the Family Support Centre - the place where I had once worked as a switchboard operator-cum-audio typist-cum-receptionist! I had applied on the off-chance because Andy had seen the advertisement in the local paper: 'Staff required to train as counsellors. A ten-week course at the end of which the trainee will hopefully gain a Certificate of Qualification, and one of three places on the counselling team, which will be based at the Family Support Unit in Bread Street, Allerton, Gaynsford. Applicants should present their CV, plus any other relevant qualifications or papers to Mike Groves, Director, Family Support Centre, Bread Street, Allerton, Gaynsford, North Midlands. Closing date...' etc., etc.

I had completed my CV and taken it along with a sheaf of letters etc., to Mike Groves, but he had not been available to see me. That day, however, he would interview me for one of the three posts within the Family Support Centre, and I was very hopeful of being successful. I wanted to work, and felt more than capable of taking on such a role; one that would be thoroughly worthwhile, keep me occupied and ensure that my brain remained active. I could feel I was becoming 'slow', and I was losing confidence stuck there in that flat in Depot Street.

Of course, it suited Andy to have me there during the day. I grinned to myself in the semi-darkness as I got out of bed and felt with my bare feet for my slippers, before wandering into the kitchen, still clad in my pyjamas, to commence preparing breakfast. Cereal was cornflakes with a sliced banana, two boiled eggs, *hard please, at least five minutes,* four half-slices of toast, and coffee, *one sugar, just a little milk.* Yes skip, anything you say, skip! I had become accustomed to my short-term role as a 'skivvy' in that flat because if I did not take the initiative and undertake most of the housework then it simply did not get done!

Andy, not to put too fine a point on it, was a slob and a slattern! Very kind, very considerate and helpful in many ways, and very caring and protective of me in some ways, but he did not like housework. He was quite happy to leave all semblance of it, i.e. cooking, washing, cleaning shoes, making beds, dusting, cleaning the bath, running his bath in the morning, making hot drinks, making sandwiches for him to take to work each day etc., etc., to his 'newfound skivvy' - me! Hitherto, I had not minded, but as I put on the kettle for tea and found his dish for his cereal, I realised that routine was beginning to pall.

I turned on the radio; Radio One. Andy liked that, although I preferred Radio Two or even Commercial Radio. The kettle was boiling. I had taken the milk out of the fridge and I stood the bottle on the side work surface whilst I carefully sliced his large banana and deposited it on top of the cornflakes before pouring on the cold milk. His eggs were boiling away and I would then toast the bread, but prior to doing that I would take the first course into the 'master bedroom' for His Lordship's consumption! I felt like James the Butler, carrying the tray and knocking on the bedroom door, waiting to be admitted, but James the Butler would be paid for his services, I wouldn't!

"Cum in, Boyzie!" called a sleepy voice.

I opened the door carefully and walked into the room, having snapped on the light by the door.

"Aw! Thanks mate! You're a jockin' star!"

Andy took the tray from me and laid it before him on the bed in which he still sat, bolt upright, waiting for his breakfast. It was just after 6.10 a.m. He had to be at work for 8 a.m., and would leave the flat at around 7 a.m. to give himself plenty of time to get there and get organised prior to starting his ten-hour shift.

"Your eggs are on, skip."

I had taken to calling him by that name and he did not seem to mind.

"Okay mate!" he responded, shoving a large spoonful of cereal and banana into his mouth.

"You know if you get this job at the Family Support Centre? Will you know today, Boyzie?"

"Yes! I hope so!" I rejoined, and went out of the room to fetch his eggs and toast, and to get myself a mug of hot strong coffee with plenty of sugar!

The day was underway, a day that could prove to be a very interesting and rewarding one for me, or not, depending on how I got on at my interview with Mike Groves that afternoon. Oh, I wanted that job! I wanted it very much indeed.

It was 6.55 a.m. and Andy had finished his breakfast, bathed, cleaned his teeth, dressed, shaved and run a comb through his hair. He was back from the newsagents at the end of the street, and reading to me prior to going off to work.

"Hey! Do you know any of these guys, Boyzie; Philip Mackie, Graham Roddis and Steven Gregson?"

I put down my mug, which was half-empty. We were sitting together on the sofa in the main living room of Andy's vast and spacious flat.

"Yeh! I went to college with all three of them, why?"

I remembered them well, Phil Mackie, Graham Roddis and Steve Gregson. They were all a little younger than me, but we had shared a dorm at Saint Mary's College in Shropshire for a term. We had got to know one another well, but they were all into sport in a far bigger way than I had ever been.

"Well, it says here in the *Echo* that three blind men, friends since their days spent together at boarding school, are planning to set out on an expedition to celebrate their 42nd birthdays and to raise money for research into ways of curing river blindness, which is prevalent in parts of Africa."

"Yes! Sounds like Phil, Graham and Steve!" I rejoined, remembering the three of them and how passionate they could become about sport and 'good causes', as they saw them!

"Yeh! Wow! They are certainly aiming high!" said Andy with real admiration in his voice. "Listen to this, Boyzie!" He read on. "To celebrate our 42nd birthdays, which all take place later this year, said Phil Mackie, we intend to raise at least £20,000 or more for the cause of research into river blindness. We intend to do this by undertaking the greatest challenge of our lives." Andy waited a moment before divulging, "They're gonna climb to the summit of Mount Kilimanjaro!

༄༅

It was the same day, Wednesday, 18 April 1990, at about 11 a.m. and I was relaxing with a cuppa prior to preparing some kind of meal for us for when Andy returned home that evening. After that, I would get ready and go out to Allerton. I had some shopping to do in town, plus Andy had left me the money and one or two bills to pay! After I had concluded my shopping spree in town, I would have lunch at the Laughing Cow before catching the bus and going on to Allerton and the Family Support Centre in Bread Street - a place of many memories for me; memories of the past, some even now too painful for me to contemplate.

I had an interview at the Family Support Centre at 3.15 p.m. with their director of services and their head of counselling services. I was a little nervous about the interview, but I would not let it show. Why on earth should I be nervous? I had worked there in the past, and some of the staff would still be there! I knew Andy would be just across the road, working shifts at the police headquarters, supporting the duty team and the family support and back-up services that the police provide in order to aid our own service. It was all very well co-ordinated and the pride of the area, the way in which our dual services complemented one another. That had always been the case, even when I had worked at the centre back in the late seventies, but since those days I had gained numerous qualifications. I had worked both as a volunteer and, more latterly, as a 'professional' in the sphere of counselling, in schools, youth custody centres and also for the homeless and rootless in the north-east of England, also for a brief period of time in Essex. No! I was foolish to get worked up about the interview. I knew in my secret heart that I would be okay, and even if I did not get one of the three places on the Stage Four Counselling Course, and thus become a qualified counsellor, it would not be the end of my world!

Waxing thus philosophical, I finished my mug of tea and washed up the pots in the sink before cleaning around the kitchen. I had done a load of washing, put it all in the spin dryer and it was now in the heating cabinet we possessed. I had had a quick dust around, but that afternoon two of Andy's sisters, Pamela and Pauline, were coming over to give the place a 'good bottoming'. They would change the beds and take the bed linen to the laundry. I was scrubbing potatoes and preparing a large saucepan and a smaller one to set on the stove, each one full of vegetables including potatoes, carrots, onion and celery, and I had taken a large steak and onion pie out of the fridge. Andy's sisters would prepare the main evening meal for me and place the plates in the oven, so all I had to do when I came home later was to warm the meal through. Good, that gave me more time to think!

So, Mac, Rod and Greg were going to celebrate their 42nd birthdays later that year by planning an expedition to climb Mount Kilimanjaro? Well, bully for them! No, I didn't mean that! Hats off to them! It was a wonderful and very daring gesture. I wished them all the good luck available to them and hoped they would raise all the money they hoped for by undertaking such a challenge. Maybe it was not actually necessary to climb a *real* mountain to prove oneself. Yes! If I could get through the interview later that day, then maybe I would be commencing my first efforts to climb up my own mountain! Maybe, with time and patience, I would be able to climb my own 'Kilimanjaro'! I had made another decision; if I was successful and managed to get the position then qualified as a counsellor, I had decided to apply to have a guide dog!

I had not told Andy! I did not know how he would react to a dog sharing the flat with us, and yet I did know that he loved animals. No, I would wait a while before mentioning it, to ensure that things were going right for me prior to implementing my decision. I mean, if I did not get the post, or qualify, there would be little or no point in my having a guide dog. I could manage to get where I wished to go, either with my white cane or with the help of Andy, other friends or relations. A guide dog would mean I could be totally independent of anyone. Yes! That certainly appealed!

Time was moving on. I finished my chores then sat for a while in the spacious lounge-cum-dining room, watching the news on TV, after which I went back into my own bedsit to endeavour to prepare for my outing and the interview, which I hoped might change the course of my life for the better.

I went into town and did some shopping then I caught the bus through to Allerton. I alighted at the stop outside James Blume's Bakery, and commenced the walk that I recalled so well. It was the walk I used to undertake almost daily, twice daily during the week, and on each and every occasion over several years, that walk had been taken along pavements and over side streets literally throng-ing with boys, youths and young men; lads from the Gunners Lane Academy and Commercial College. I still saw many of them in those days, although not as often as I used to do. Time marches on! People move on to different places and into different spheres of life, but loads and loads of them still lived in the area and I was fortunate enough to know many of them and their families. It was like a 'brotherhood' that had never really broken up.

I walked on quickly, my head full of memories. Andy and a whole army of his mates were sitting in the bar of the Gunners in Allerton, enjoying a substantial lunch. Father Martyn McCallasky had joined them, along with Father Bernard and Father Dominic, the three senior priests at Saint Jude's. The three tables, crowded with blokes and one policewoman, DS Jane Bonnier, were rocking with laughter. Andy had just come to the end of a very long and extremely vulgar joke!

"Coor lummie!" exclaimed Harry Devaney. "Yo' dun't get ony better f'r keepin', that's for sure, Andy!"

Jane Bonnier sipped at her half pint of lager and grinned. Jane was a lesbian. She had a partner, DI Nora Scott. Jane and Nora had lived together for some ten years, and they were the life and soul of any parties given by members of the Force. No decent party was complete without Nora and Jane!

"So, you'll all cum on Saturday night then?" said Andy, downing his pint in one gulp and ordering a second.

"Oh ahr!" agreed everyone around the three tables.

Andy smirked.

"The place will be packed! It'll be a real blast! Aw'm really lookin' forward to it, guys!"

"And gals," said Jane, playfully.

Everyone laughed.

"We dun't fink of yo' as a gal, Sarge, ye're one o' the lads!" said Fred Wynter, a young detective constable, recently promoted from the 'ranks', and on his probationary term of duty at the police headquarters, south division.

Everyone laughed boisterously, but good-naturedly.

"It'll be gud to see Boyzie again! Aw knew him when he was a lot younger!" said Joe Capper.

Nods, winks, nudges and other similar signs were exchanged among the cops packed around the three tables, and Father Martyn grinned. Andy Bold, a big cop with ginger hair and a fine full beard, spoke.

"Yeh, aw remember the story!"

Joe Capper's big shoulders sagged, he shuffled his feet beneath the table and downed his second pint. Joe had been of assistance to Boyzie on that fateful day when he had been pushed out in front of an oncoming truck while he stood waiting at the junction of Gunners Lane and Hyland Road. It was the morning of that day in May 1978, when his late wife, Susan, had been admitted to the County Hospital for the last time. Joe scowled at Andy Bold, who smirked behind his hands and finished his own pint. At least, thought Joe, aw was there when he needed me. Yeh! On two different occasions, I was there to help Boyzie. He consoled himself with that thought and pushed his empty tankard to the other end of the cluttered table.

The party around the three tables was beginning to break up. Everyone had to get back to work, so the lunch break was over and duties recommenced. Everyone felt a bit more like it now that they had a drink or two and a substantial pub lunch inside their bellies.

"We ought to get dahn the health an' fitness centre sometime," said Andy Bold as a crowd of the guys walked back to the police headquarters together.

"Yeh, aw'd like that!" agreed Andy Gange, who had put on weight ever since being discharged from the hospital.

Boyzie's good cooking and regular meals were the reason for that - he knew it! His sisters and his mom, and even his owd gran, were also always baking, so he and Boyzie had plenty of cakes, pies, trifles etc., to enjoy, and the fridge and the freezer were always well stocked. Boyzie had become quite a hit with Andy's vast family. His mother adored him and his gran, who lived just around the corner from his mom, also had a 'soft spot for the lad'. His eight sisters and four brothers, plus their partners and children, thought he was great, and he had fitted in real well with Andy's very large and extremely boisterous family.

The other tenants in the flats seemed to have taken to Boyzie too, and the people in the locality around the flats in Depot Street spoke well of him. Now it was time to introduce Boyzie to his armies of mates, and see how he went down with them, and they with him, of course! Yes! Andy was looking forward to the 'big bash' on Saturday. The place would be packed out, stacked out with people and pulsating with life! He hadn't had a good bash in ages, and it would make the world of difference to everyone to let their hair down, play the fool a bit etc., etc. Yes, and let his lodger into what was about to occur!

5

I T WAS strange, once again walking down towards the junction of Gunners Lane. The memories came flooding back to me as I drew near the crossing, *that* crossing where it had all begun on that fateful day in May 1978.

Like vast armies of ghosts, they seemed to throng around me, to follow after me, to dog my every step in such a vastness of numbers! I could almost hear their voices; the deep, sonorous, earth-shattering roar, surmounted by the shrill, high-pitched cacophonous tumult of falsetto voices:

"Boyzie! Boyzie! We're all arrahnd yo', mate! Dun't worry, Boyzie! We'll look after yo', mate!"

I steadied myself and cursed myself for being a stupid fool! It was the wind blowing down the street, whistling through the ether all around me, as I set my feet upon the road that led towards the Family Support Centre on Bread Street. It was the tenth street on the right, off Gunners Lane, the building being set back at the end of a short concrete driveway. Yes! Ah yes! The memories came flooding back.

I stood for a few moments at the end of that concrete driveway, the driveway leading up to the entrance of the Family Support Centre, and remembered another occasion when I had stood there, an occasion some 12 years before, around the middle of May, an occasion when I had been surrounded by the 'network' of young people, who later supported and helped me so much and so often over the coming weeks and months, nay years! I remembered telling them all about the loss of my late wife, Susan. I recalled how they had listened, stunned into silence - a heavy, all-pervading silence that enveloped us all, and wrapped itself around us like a mantle. I remembered Thomas Paul Copley, who was now married with several kids, and who worked at the Heath Road Health and Fitness Centre, placing a hand on my shoulder and encouraging me to talk to them about my situation.

"Go on Boyzie! We're all listenin', mate!"

When I had finished they had literally mobbed me as I stood at the end of the driveway. How they had pushed, jostled, almost fought with one another to stand beside me, to shake my hands, to press their young bodies against mine and put their arms around or across my shoulders, anything to show their solidarity as one with me in my time of sorrow.

"Dun't worry, mate. We're here for you! You're a gud bloke. We like you, Boyzie! We'll look after yo', mate!"

I could feel my face becoming hot. Oh no! I did not want to show any signs of raw emotion. Not at that moment, not there!

"Hi!"

I almost jumped out of my skin! I had been so preoccupied that I had not heard anyone approach.

"Are you okay?"

I half-turned.

"Oh yes, I'm... I'm just going into the Family Support Centre - I've got an interview later."

"For the post of counsellor?"

The man who stood beside me on my right appeared to be very tall, and he had a very strong American accent.

"Yeh! That's right, mate!" I rejoined.

"Same here!" he said, and then, "glad to know you. I'm Otis Hyram McKinley Masher, I'm holding out my hand."

I shivered slightly. Those were some of the words my darling Sue had said to me the first time we were introduced to one another at Saint Mary's College in Shropshire - 'I'm holding out my hand'. I extended my hand to the guy standing on my right.

27

"Ian Richard Dickson," I said, smiling politely, "known to all as Boyzie!"

"Hi Boyzie!" rejoined Masher. "Shall we go in together?"

That was how I first met Otis Hyram McKinley Masher of Plymouth County, New England, USA, as I was standing outside the gateway to the Family Support Centre, where we would both end up working, but I am running ahead of myself again! One step at a time, Boyzie, one step at a time, mate!

6

Summary of Events - January 1979 to midsummer 1979.

AFTER THE New Year's Party at the end of 1978, and the revelation imparted to me in the early hours of a cold frosty morning - the first morning of the New Year - the revelation that Sandy Christmas was pregnant and that I was the father of her expected child, my life became exceedingly complicated for a while. As soon as I was able, I left Sandy and her family in Harts Hill, in the north-east, and returned home to Gaynsford. Sandy had not wanted me to go with me.

"You'll cum back again won't you, my love?" she had whined as I was leaving in a taxi to go to Harts Hill Station to catch the train down to Brigthorpe!

I thanked Sandy politely for her hospitality over the New Year, but said that in all probability I would not be back for some time, adding, in my head, 'I may not be back at all'.

"But, Boyzie, you must cum back to me!" she whined on. "You are the father of my expected child! I know you are, Boyzie, an' now I've told you, well... you've got responsibilities towards me an' the baby I'm expecting, so... so you've *got* to cum back to me!"

I told her I would have to consider all possibilities, and that taking all things into account, I did not believe I was the father of the child she was expecting. Yes, we had indulged in lovemaking as we lay together beneath the trees in Donkey Meadow on that bright, sunny Sunday afternoon towards the end of August 1978, but well… I did not believe it could have occurred like that. Our lovemaking on that occasion had been hasty, not steady and slow, but quick, fumbling, almost as though we were ashamed of what we were doing, or afraid that we would be caught out doing it!

No! I did not believe she was pregnant by me, and my thoughts as I travelled home to Gaynsford on that Wednesday, 3rd January 1979, were jumbled and confused. If I *was* the father of her anticipated child then by rights I ought to marry her, but I did not love her and I did not want to marry her. Of course, I cared for her, as a friend, and I thought the world of the four kids, but that wasn't enough on which to base a long-term relationship. No, no, I could not - I *would* not marry Sandy Christmas, yet how could I turn my back upon her and her family if indeed I really was the expected child's father? Oh God! What a bloody mess! I was so engrossed in thinking about my situation that I nearly missed my stop at Brigthorpe, where I had to change to catch the 'down train' to Gaynsford.

On arrival home, I was met outside the station at Gaynsford by a large crowd of Rob McCallasky's mates. Father Martyn, the priest and cousin of my late friend, had come down to the railway station with a horde of Rob's brothers, cousins etc., and stacks of his mates to meet a vast contingent of Irish relatives who were over there for the memorial service, which was to take place at Saint Jude's Roman Catholic Church in Allerton on Saturday, 6th January.

Martyn saw me and gave a loud whoop of joy.

"Hey, Boyzie!" he roared, and he rushed to me and flung his arms around me. "It's great that you're home, mate. You'll be able to come to his memorial service then?"

He practically danced me over to where the vast crowd was waiting for us! I was surrounded, and hastily introduced to all Rob's relations from the Emerald Isle, who had so far arrived for the service. Blokes and women were queuing to shake my hands, to pat me on the back and on the shoulders. Maura O'Reilly, who had virtually been brought up with the McCallasky family, but whom had eventually returned to live at home with her own family in Ireland, had been like a sister to Rob. She was a small, petite Brunette with fire in her eyes. "Sure, I'm so delighted to meet you, Boyzie!" she exclaimed. "Sure, and didn't our Rob speak about yez aal de toime, so he did. An' it was all gud, so it was, Boyzie!"

Everyone collected up cases, bags and rucksacks, and we all trouped into the Station Hotel, just around the corner from Gaynsford Parkway, and had a drink or two altogether. It was good to be home and once more among friends and members of the 'network'. We sat, drank and talked well into the late evening; myself and Father Martyn, Des, Brendan and Eddie, more brothers and cousins of Rob, plus lots of his mates and other relatives who had arrived that day from Ireland. A rowdy raucous crowd they were indeed, but very friendly and even protective towards me, at least so it seemed to me anyway.

Maura O'Reilly's brother, Sheamus, was a bit of a hooligan, and we endeavoured to keep him out of trouble! He almost got involved in a couple of fights, but his sister, his brother, Niall, and his cousins, Rory and Eammon, managed to keep him under control with a mixture of cajolement and threatening! In the end, we all left the Station Hotel and piled, together with all our luggage, into four minibuses, several cabs and Father Martyn's old van, and drove back to my place!

It was the early hours of the morning before most people left and either went back to Rob's mother's house or to other relations or friends in the Allerton and Osleston areas of the town! I unpacked my luggage and had a bath before laying down for a couple of hours on the put-you-up sofa I had recently acquired for the front room.

ॐ

At around 6.45 a.m. the following morning, Thursday, I was up and tidying around before eating a bowl of cereal and getting showered, shaved and ready for work. The New Year break was over and it was time to get back into the 'old routine'.

I had learned that Rob's memorial service was due to take place at Saint Jude's on Saturday, 6th January at 3.30 p.m. and, of course, I intended to be there. I had also made the offer to Father Martyn and to others that on the Friday night, as indeed it had been on the night prior to Rob's funeral, it would be open house at mine for anyone who wished to come and be with me to remember Rob, talk about him, listen to his favourite music, readings etc., etc., and just remember his life. Maudlin? I did not think so. Prior to Rob's funeral my house had been packed out with his relations and mates; we had all drawn comfort and consolation from one another. Now, the same plan could be adhered to prior to his memorial service if people wished to avail themselves of the opportunity for quiet contemplation, or a chance to talk to others about Rob, his life, his 'deeds of daring do' etc., etc. Martyn said he would let everyone know and was sure that people would flock to my house that coming Friday evening, so I thought I had better make preparations for their arrival!

As I got ready for work that morning, the morning of the first Thursday in January 1979, my first day back at work since the New Year break, I could hear a great deal of noise coming from the house at the end of the close - number 25 - the house that used to be the home of the Williams family. The new inhabitants of the property were Bessie and Jim Starling, and their offspring. A large and chaotic family, they were extremely noisy, at times to the point of near bedlam! I believed that Jim knocked his wife about, and knew that some of the kids were real trouble magnets, especially their son, Malcolm, a tough little cookie, who, although he was always good humoured and pleasant whenever he spoke to me, had a bad reputation in the neighbourhood as a tearaway.

That morning the noise ensuing from the house next door at the end of the close bordered on the bedlamic! I could hear screams, a good deal of swearing, yells from the younger children, doors slamming and then something smashing hard up against the wall.

I stood stock still, listening for a moment, wondering if I ought to knock, but eventually decided not to bother, merely to get on with what I had to do and get out of my house before the situation became completely out of control and I had to intervene. Coward? No, no I'm not, but well... you know! Like so many of us at that time, on that Thursday, raw, cold January morning, I did not want to become involved in the affairs of my neighbours.

I went upstairs, having finished my breakfast and my last cup of tea, and finished getting ready for work. As I stood in the bedroom tying my tie, I heard a tremendous racket ensuing from the house next door. Jim, my male neighbour, was roaring his heart out, while his wife, Bessie, literally screamed for mercy! It sounded to me as though Jim was cracking Bessie's head against the wall while shouting abuse at her. In the background, the dog was barking fit to beat the band, while several children screamed and cried themselves into near hysteria! Oh, my God! I could not go out to work and leave a situation like that going on next door. I had to do something! I toyed with the idea of going around there, but instead, decided to phone the police.

I went towards my bedside table and the shelf that held my telephone, when suddenly there was an urgent ring at the door. I rushed downstairs, half-dressed, to see who was outside. I had hardly opened the front door when Malcolm Starling, closely followed by several of his younger siblings, rushed into my house! The kids were almost hysterical with fear.

"Oh! Oh, Boyzie!" yelled Malcolm, blundering into the hallway and almost falling into my outstretched arms. "Can yo' ring the polis, quickly Boyzie! Aw fink..." He was shaking. "Aw fink me dad's jus' killed me mam!"

Bessie Starling had been battered and kicked to death by her drunken bully of a husband! Jim was an alcoholic, who kept bottles of booze hidden in the house in cupboards, sheds at the bottom of the garden etc., and drank himself stupid most of the time. He had worked as a coalman when he first moved into the close. Indeed, on the day he and his family had moved in, they had arrived on a coal lorry, much to the amusement of me and my late mate, Rob McCallasky, who had been staying with me overnight and had witnessed their arrival.

I had never really had a great deal to do with either Bessie or Jim, but I knew most of the children by name, and often spoke to Malcolm, who had been around to my house on several occasions. Jim had killed his wife, Bessie, in front of most of their children! There were eight children living with them in the house at the time! Their eldest daughter, Carol, was married and already had three children of her own, despite only being 19 years of age. After Jim's arrest for murder, and his subsequent trial and life sentence, I never saw or heard of any of the Starling family again. I know that Malcolm and Dennis, the two eldest lads, went to live with their married sister, and the other children, six of them including one daughter, were taken into care and placed in foster homes.

Our small close and the surrounding area became a media circus for a while after the terrible tragedy of 4th January 1979, and the house at number 25 was fumigated, had the guts torn out of it, and was completely redecorated, re-wired etc., etc., over a period of more than a year. Despite all that, still nobody wanted to live there!

After what had transpired on that dreadful day in Rutland Close, Parkside, Gaynsford, the proposed memorial service for the late Rob McCallasky did not take place as planned on 6th January. His hordes of relations went back to Ireland, a new date was set for Saturday, 14th April, and it was decided that instead of holding the service in Gaynsford, it would take place over in Ireland, where Rob's grandmother and most of his aunts, uncles, cousins etc., still lived.

Father Martyn, who had become a personal friend of mine, visited me and asked if I would like to go over with him, plus Rob's mam and at least 40 other members of his family, also about 100 of his pals! I was honoured! I told Martyn that of course I would love to go over to Ireland and see where the McCallasky family had lived, and where my late, and still lamented, mate had called 'home'. Rob had been born over in the Emerald Isle, but his parents had moved to England soon after his birth.

On Thursday, 12th April 1979, we flew from Flixton Airport in the north-west, over to Dublin then travelled by road on to County Mahon, and the town of Kilgallen. We stayed with one of Father Martyn's sisters, Gronia, plus her vast clan, and were made very welcome by everyone in the town.

The memorial service for Rob was very well attended, in fact the Church of Saint Agnes was extremely full, so full that they had to relay the service to the crowds outside who could not gain entrance! All the main participants - his mother, brothers and sisters, plus all other family members and loads of his mates - were present in the crowded church, and Father Martyn took part in the two-hour Mass for my late and greatly revered friend, whose loss I still felt most acutely. Dear Rob! He had been a source of great pleasure and amusement in my life during the brief period of time I had been privileged to know him. Like poor Bessie Starling, I hoped sincerely that Rob would now rest in peace.

I decided I liked Kilgallen, where the people were so warm and friendly, and where life seemed to be that much more slow and steady than it was over in England. Time did not seem to matter in the same way as it always did in Gaynsford. Of course, people worked and lived normal lives - even busy lives - but somehow their attitude to life and time and everything in general seemed much more laid-back, and the feeling was definitely infectious.

I enjoyed my time with Martyn's sister, Gronia, and her large family, and also I enjoyed my newfound relationship with Maura O'Reilly. Maura was lovely, bubbly, full of life, full of brogue and bunkum! I loved her at first meeting, and she seemed to be very fond of me too, but I did not need any more complications in my life at that time. No, I did not! An involvement with yet another woman in my life would certainly have been an added problem!

Maura was like a breath of fresh air wafting through my days. Her presence infected my whole existence and made me sing with a new joy that I had not felt for some considerable time. I kept telling myself, 'Steady Boyzie! She's not for you! You can't take on yet another female in your complex life at present, you have enough on with Johnnie Friscoe, Sandy Christmas and also Honey Laverne'. I certainly had not forgotten Honey!

It was easier said than done to turn away from the charms and pleasures of the company of that very vivacious, bubbly, happy-go-lucky woman, who adored me and went out of her way to try and ensure that she was always in my company. I was not protesting! No, not by any means, rather, I sought her company too, and longed for the times when we were together - especially if we were alone together! Oh yes, Maura O'Reilly was a little witch, and the witch was weaving her spells, which were certainly working upon me! 'Come into my parlour,' said the spider to the fly!

We have been here before!

7

I N THE early part of June 1979, Sandy Christmas gave birth to a ten pound daughter! I was at work at the Family Support Unit and the telephone rang. It was Norma Townley, Sandy's cousin. She told me Sandy had had a baby daughter, and she was going to call her Belle, after her mother. I offered my congratulations, and Norma put the phone down on me.

A couple of weeks later I went up to Harts Hill to stay with Doreen, Fred and their tribe! Doreen, my sister, was married to Fred Dingle, who was in charge of the vast pig breeding unit based at the farm that used to belong to Dan Daley. Dan and his wife no longer had the farm under their jurisdiction, although they kept a degree of interest in what went on there. Their son and his family were the new owners of the farm and they thought the world of 'ahr Fred', David Frederick Dingle, my brother-in-law.

During the course of my three weeks' sojourn in Harts Hill, I visited Sandy Christmas and met the new arrival, the child she was convinced was my daughter! Belle was a bonny little girl, chubby and robust, with a good pair of lungs on her and a voracious appetite.

"She always wants feeding," whined Sandy.

That was a trait I had always detested in her; her whiney voice when she wanted someone to feel sorry for her.

"I don't know what the problem is with you," I told her one afternoon while visiting for tea and to see the kids. "You've got a smashing little family, a nice house, you do pretty well for friends and yet you are always miserable!"

"Ooh! That's not fair, Boyzie!" she said, with some essence of emotion and a degree of forcefulness in her voice, for a change. "You knaw why I get upset when yo' are around! Aw... aw still luv yo', darlin', an'... an aw wanna-"

I cut her short.

"Sandy! You are a nice girl, and I appreciate your friendship. I enjoy your company and I love the kids to death, but Sandy, I can't marry you, no, or even live with you. It would never work, love, and that's that and all about it, as my Grannie Annie would say!"

We had tears then, at least for a while, but I pretended to take no notice and eventually I went off into the garden with the kids to play a game of football, or 'socca', as little Dylan used to call it! When I left Sandy and her family on that Thursday evening, it was the last time I saw them, but I understand that Belle, the new baby, died a cot death in the November of 1979, just a few months after her birth. Naturally Sandy was devastated, but she never contacted me about it. I had letters from Doreen and also Norma Townley, both telling me the sad details. Apparently the local paper had been full of it. Sandy and her family subsequently left Harts Hill and moved down to Marsh End to live near her mother, and I believe Sandy helped her to run a grocery and general store in the seaside town on the south coast. Exit Sandy Christmas and her family from my life, which in effect was just as well because by then I had a new girlfriend - Maura O'Reilly!

Maura and I saw a great deal of one another following our visit to Ireland and the memorial service held at the Church of Saint Agnes for the late Rob McCallasky. I had loved it over there, and couldn't wait to return to the town of Kilgallen, where the people were so friendly and life was so laid-back compared with the hectic life I led whilst I was in Gaynsford. When Father Martyn suggested we went back over there in the late Summer of 1979, I immediately acquiesced. We had a wonderful time, staying with many of Martyn's relatives, and Maura accompanied me on many wonderful outings to places with fabulous names, to country pubs and bars in towns, which were like shanty towns, or towns out of Wild West shows in the movies! I loved it all, and I loved it more because of the presence of Maura O'Reilly!

We spent three glorious weeks over there, and as we drove to the airport to fly home, Maura made a promise to me that she would be over for Christmas. I flew home with my head in a daze, foolish lad that I was, bringing yet another woman into my life at that time, but Sandy Christmas was now out of the picture!

I had not been back to Glosport since the death of Rob on that fateful night the previous November, so I had seen nothing of Honey Laverne. Incredibly, since her stay with me at Christmas the previous year, and one phone call just before the New Year and my departure for Harts Hill, I had seen and heard nothing from Johnnie Friscoe! All that was to change very soon!

8

Wednesday, 18th April 1990 - 6.10 p.m.

I WAS STILL at the Family Support Unit in Allerton. I had been there since just after 3 p.m. that afternoon, when I had entered the building with my new friend, Otis McKinley Masher, from Plymouth County, New England in the USA, who had only been over in England for just under four months and had just come to live in Gaynsford. In fact, he told me that he had not yet moved entirely as he still had many of his 'goods and shackles' down in the flat he was sharing in London!

"If I am lucky, and I get this job," he told me, "I'll look for somewhere up here to live, but, until I know if I've been successful, well, I may as well stay where I am, I reckon!"

We were sitting together in a large comfortable room at the end of an extension of the building, which had not existed when I worked there back in 1978. There were eight of us waiting to know whether or not we had been successful in our interviews that afternoon. It had been a very busy and extremely interesting afternoon. To begin with, as we entered the reception area I was greeted by familiar voices.

"Aw! It's Boyzie! See! It's ahr Boyzie cum back to us!"

To the surprise of Otis Masher, who still stood beside me awaiting entry into the main building, three women rushed out through the doorway marked 'Reception' and each one embraced and kissed me hard, two on the side of my face and one full on the lips! It was Sandra Couchman, Mandy Moss, now Mandy Blythe, and Tina Jobling, who had been the office junior when I worked there before. All three women were delighted to see me, as indeed was Alison Hockley, who had been one of the clerk typists and had joined the staff during the late Autumn of 1978. We were hustled through the doorway and I was taken into the office that had originally been Chris Braun's domain, and offered a cup of tea! Otis was shown through to the large room in which we now sat, along with other candidates, but I was given that bit of 'special' treatment because they knew me and wanted to know all my news!

I was told that Pat Lenham had left. She apparently had two more children and was happy to be at home caring for her family at that time. I met Barbara Mills and Ann Nolan, who were new additions to the staff, and also made the acquaintance of Ben Marcello once more.

"Hey-up, Boyzie!" said Ben, now middle-aged, balding and rather overweight for a bloke of his height. "Great to see you again, mate!"

I really did feel very welcome, and was more than happy as I chatted away to members of the staff whom I had known in the past. At around 3.15 p.m., Mike Grove's secretary, Diane Jarvis, came into the office and asked me to go with her to Mike's room, where the interview would be conducted. Diane seemed very pleasant, if a little harassed. We walked together to the office of the new director of services, Mr Mike Groves. Diane and I entered Mike's office and he immediately stood up and came across to shake my hand. Also in the office with him were Mr Christopher Braun, the director of administrative services, Wayne Clark, the leader of the counselling team and his deputy, Shirley Beresford. I shook hands with them all and Chris and Wayne both said how very pleased they were to see me!

"Please take a seat, Ian - or perhaps I may call you Boyzie?" asked Mike Groves, who had a very strong South African accent.

The interview lasted for just over an hour, and I was fielding questions from all four of them! I believed I did pretty well, though. I felt good! I felt confident! My welcome had been so very warm, and I had a glow of pleasure and excitement inside me at the end of my discussion with Mike Groves and his staff on that warm and pleasant April afternoon. It had been a long day for them. They had started at just before 9.15 a.m. and some of the candidates had been there all day. One or two were becoming restless! I think nerves were beginning to get the better of them.

After my interview, Chris Braun guided me back to the main waiting room and he was able to get me a mug of hot chocolate from the newly installed drinks machine. It was hot and wet, although not very pleasant, but I needed it all the same after the rigors and traumas of the long and quite gruelling interview I had just been through.

Chris Braun was now married and had two daughters. He lived in Osleston. Three of his younger brothers had been married, although two of them, John and Jim, were now divorced and living back at home with their mam. Their dad, another Jim, had died two years before of cancer. The two youngest lads, Steve and Kev, both still lived at home. Chris and his brother, Phil, were the only ones still married. Apparently the family had moved to a three bedroom council dwelling on the Heath Road Estate, opposite Heath Road Primary School.

Chris was delighted to see me and told me, as he sat beside me drinking a mug of hot sweet coffee, he was sure I had done well during the interview. I said I hoped he was right! I really wanted that job more than ever. We were all chatting in the large waiting room, which we later discovered was the staffroom, and drinking from big brown mugs, when Diane Jarvis came into the room holding a sheaf of papers in her right hand.

"Mike and Chris will be here in a moment." she declared. "They'll tell you the results of the interviews and of everything that you undertook today."

She closed the door, and we all finished our drinks. My hands were shaking! I was sitting between Otis Masher, who seemed very cool, calm and collected, and a very voluble, although like-able, Welsh bloke called Wes Pritchard. He came from Tiger Bay in Cardiff, and seemed very friendly, although rather nervous. He was 41 years old and was currently employed as a prison officer at a remand centre in South Wales. He was also very hopeful of landing a job, as we all hoped very hard for one another, as well as for ourselves, the three of us, Wes, Otis and me.

We had also been captivated by the bravery of a young woman, very attractive and pleasant, by the name of Liz Lane. Liz was in a wheelchair. She had spina bifida, and had been working as a teacher at Thorney Close Primary School at the other end of town. It was an establishment very well known to me, and had a special needs department in which Liz had been working. She was unhappy in that environment, and did not feel fulfilled. She had great hopes of procuring a position at the Family Support Unit on Bread Street, Allerton.

Time passed. At just after 6.30 p.m. the door to the staffroom opened and Mick Groves, Chris Braun, plus Wayne Clark and Shirley Beresford, came trouping in! They all sat down. When all was still, Mike Groves spoke in his quiet, but authoritative voice with his broad, musical South African annunciation.

"We've decided to appoint four of you to post, rather than three. We are sorry that some of you will be disappointed, but feel very happy to offer posts to the following persons - Miss Eliza Joy Lane, Mr Otis Mckinley Masher, Mr Wesley George Pritchard and Mr Ian George Dickson. Congratulations to all four of you. If the rest of you will see Mr Braun as you leave, he will ensure that you receive any expenses incurred during your journey and also any other expenditure for which you are claiming. I would like to thank you all very much for attending today, and I am sorry it's been such a long day for some of you. Would those I have named please remain behind just for a few more minutes, so that we can settle expenses with you etc., etc. Thanks again for your patience today."

"Well done!" said Otis Masher as he took my right hand and

squeezed it hard in a gesture of friendliness.

I was almost in tears, but they were tears of happiness! I had done it! I was commencing my ascent of my own Mount Kilimanjaro!

9

O N THAT evening, the evening of Wednesday, 18th April
1990, I went home walking on clouds nine, ten and
climbing onto eleven! I had been so convinced that I
would not be successful in obtaining that position as a trainee
counsellor, even though it was the venue in which I had worked
successfully for some time in the past. Lo and behold, I had been
successful, and a week on the following Monday, 30th April 1990,
I would be commencing work – no, I would be *recommencing*
work at my old venue, but that time I would have a new and much
more exciting role to play within the organisation.

I was so very thrilled and excited at the prospect that night that
I could have taken on anything that came my way, or at least that's
what I thought until I arrived back at Andy's flat and discovered
the current situation!

I walked to the bus stop with Otis McKinley Masher, with
whom I had been chatting for most of the afternoon when we had
been waiting around in the staffroom between interviews, and
with whom I was gradually building up a friendship, a friendship
that would prove to be long-lasting and of great value to me in the
future, but at the time I did not realise it.

"So, we both made it eh, Boyzie?" he said as we arrived together
at the bus stop.

It was the bus stop where I had often waited of an evening, surrounded by members of the vast 'network' of youngsters who had
plagued my life and thronged my footsteps and my every waking

moment when I was working in that area, but all that was in the past! Wasn't it? I shivered slightly.

"Yeh! Great, isn't it?" I said with feeling.

"Yeh! I'm sure looking forward to starting work there, I reckon it's gonna be okay working there, an' everyone seems so friendly, don't you think so, Boyzie?" said Masher, shuffling his feet as he stood beside me awaiting the arrival of the bus into town.

I agreed.

"Of course, I know some of the staff from when I worked there before, you know," I said, and proceeded to tell him how I had worked there as the receptionist-cum-switchboard operator-cum-audio typist during the seventies.

"Gee, that's really interesting, Boyzie! So, you've got inside information on the place eh?"

I laughed.

"Anything you want to know, just ask your Uncle Boyzie!" I said, then the bus arrived and we were clambering on board.

We sat together at the back of the vehicle, and we chatted amicably until it was time to get off in town. We went our separate ways, but first of all I told McKinley Masher where I was living and issued a cordial invitation for him to visit any time he wished to do so.

"Gee thanks, Boyzie, I may well take you up on that, pal!" he said, as he warmly shook my hand, then he had gone, and I was walking along towards Depot Street and the flat where I lived with my new mate, Andy Gange.

As I turned onto Depot Street it occurred to me that it would not have hurt Andy to call in at the Family Support Unit to meet me that evening, after all, he knew I was going to be there. Still, maybe he thought I would have been home by now. Ah well! It didn't matter anyway, as I was home now. I unlocked the front door and as I walked into the main hallway I could smell meals cooking in the various flats. I suddenly felt very guilty, although for the life of me I did not know why. I had no reason to feel guilty! I had been out, and I had been for an interview, and Andy was quite as capable as I was of preparing a meal. I doubted very much that he would have bothered to turn his hand to doing so, however, and of course, as I entered the flat we shared I was deemed right in every respect.

I almost fell over Andy's shoes in the hallway. Great! I walked into the kitchen, put the kettle on and lit the gas under the two saucepans that I had left on the stove that morning. They were both almost full to the brim with potatoes, carrots, leeks, onions, celery etc. That would be a start anyway! I could hear the water in the shower running, and guessed that Andy was in there. Lazy beggar! How did he imagine things got done? Did he think it all just happened, that the place just cleaned and tidied itself maybe? I felt a little angry as I found the large pie I had left in its dish, and lit the oven to cook it through. I turned the oven up high and reckoned to give the pie about 25 to 30 minutes to cook, perhaps a little longer. It was a very large steak and onion pie, and it would be a very big dinner that I was now in process of preparing. I placed the pie on the middle shelf of the oven, which was heating up nicely, and was in process of pouring the tea into two large, brown earthenware mugs when Andy emerged from the shower.

"Aw! Hi Boyzie! Fancy cummin' in wi' me, mate?"

I was shocked - stunned into silence - and all the more so when I realised he was dead serious! Andy had never spoken to me like that before, in all the time we had known one another.

"No!" I exclaimed. "I'm getting the dinner ready, making the tea etc., and then I want a shower too. I'm all hot and sticky."

"Aw! Cum in the shower wi' me! I'll soon cool you dahn, mate!" he said.

He kicked off his slippers and came to stand behind me in his bare feet. He began to massage my shoulders. Frankly, I was unsure how to react to that overture on his part.

"No! No Andy, please don't do that!"

He moved away with a sigh, and went and sat down in the large living area of the flat, which we shared. He was clad in a dressing gown, slippers and pyjama bottoms, and he smelled of strong aftershave, shampoo, scented soap and toothpaste.

"Meal nearly ready?" he asked gruffly.

"No!" I rejoined. "I've not been in long, but it won't take long to sort it all. You just sit there and relax!"

I managed to put a degree of sarcasm into the last statement, and it did not go unnoticed.

"Wot's up, mate?" Andy asked in a more friendly tone.

I did not reply immediately, as I was stirring the tea in the mugs. I took one through and handed it to him.

"Nothing! At least there wasn't until…"

I stopped in front of him where he was lounging on the sofa and he took the mug of tea from my shaking hands.

"Fanks Boyzie! Until wot?" he asked, taking a long swig from the big brown earthenware mug.

"I'm not your bloody skivvy, Andy! I don't mind doing things around the flat, but I… I don't care to be taken for granted!"

Suddenly I could feel my face getting hot. I had opened the floodgates, so now it would all come out.

"Boyzie!" His tone was dangerous. "If you've got summat to say, then let's hear it!"

Yes! Yes, I had plenty to say, but I was not ready to say it yet.

"It will keep" I said, and went back into the kitchen to pour myself another mug of tea and to finish getting our huge meal ready.

He rose from the sofa where he had been sprawling, and followed me into the kitchen in his bare feet, standing behind me once more as I lifted the kettle from the stove. He slipped his arm around my shoulders and pulled me to him! I was so shocked I almost dropped the scalding water from the brimming kettle all over my feet.

"Christ Andy! What the jockin' hell are you doing?" I yelled as realisation dawned upon me and I thought of what could have occurred if I had not immediately reacted to prevent the inevitable.

"Go and sit down and I'll bring you your meal and another drink when everything is ready. It won't be two ticks now!"

He remained standing behind me, his elbows resting on my shoulders.

"Did you not get that job then?" he asked.

"*Actually, I did!*" I shouted, thinking that at last he had deigned to remember where I had been. "So you will soon be losing your skivvy 'cos I'll be out at work during the day! Sorry and all that, but there it is. Now, shift yourself, I'm busy!"

I was bloody angry, and he knew it! I really believed he realised he had gone that step too far. He went back into the living area and flung himself down on the put-you-up sofa again. I closed the kitchen door, poured myself a second mug of hot strong tea and stood by the back door drinking it. I was totally engrossed in my own thoughts, and did not hear the pad, pad of bare feet as Andy came up behind me yet again. I did not realise he was there until his arms encircled my body and I felt him trying to squeeze the very breath out of me!

I staggered, the big brown earthenware mug flew from my hand and smashed on the yard, and I fell forwards. I had more or less finished my tea, so I was not badly scalded, but some hot liquid poured down over my hands. Andy pulled me into his arms and began to ruffle my hair! He was behaving quite roughly with me and I was very afraid.

"Don't you ever talk to me like I was rubbish, Boyzie! Aw'm not jockin' rubbish, mate, an' yo' owe me for havin' allowed yo' to move in wiv me, so dun't stand there cummin' the jockin' innocent wi' me! Yo' owe me big time, Boyzie, an' aw wun't let you forget it neither!"

I knew he meant it. He banged my head against the door frame and then turned around and left me sprawling on the floor in the doorway on my hands and knees. Bastard! The heartless little bastard! I stayed where I was for a while until I heard him moving about in the living area, then I hauled myself carefully to my feet and went through to my own bedsit. I lay on the bed for a while, and buried my face in the pillows. The tears came hot and freely - tears of anger, tears of utter frustration.

I was being used, and I was not prepared to put up with it for long. No way! I was worth more than that wasn't I? I lay there on the bed, shaking. How long did I lie on that bed, my head buzzing, my face buried in the pile of pillows? Was it ten minutes, an hour? I did not know! I seemed to have lost all conception of time, but as I lay there, I could feel my whole body trembling, shaking with sobs. Stupid! Stupid, crass idiot to place my trust in someone whom I hardly knew! To believe I could move into a flat with another bloke and share with him, and that everything would be perfect just because we had got along well when we were together in a hospital ward, did not mean we could rub along together all day every day in a domestic situation like sharing a flat. No! I was an idiot to have believed it would all be okay and that it would all work out right.

I must have cried myself into a fitful slumber! The next thing I remembered, I felt myself being gently shaken by the shoulders - not roughly, but gently - and a calm, rational voice was talking quietly and easily.

"Boyzie, Boyzie, wake up, mate."

I lifted my aching head from the pile of pillows and turned over onto my back on the bed where I still lay. Andy, clad in pyjama bottoms and socks, sat down on the bed beside me and reached to take my left hand, which lay on the quilt. I did not draw away.

"Boyzie!" he said, and his voice sounded choked. "I'm… I'm sorry, mate, I didn't mean to hit you, Boyzie, I can't imagine what came over me! Cum through to the living area, mate! I've cooked the meal and it's ready to serve. I've bin out while you've bin asleep, an' bought a couple of quart bottles of cider. They are in the fridge cooling. Cum on, Boyzie! I'm real sorry, mate, I wouldn't hurt you for the world, you know that don't you, Boyzie?"

He squeezed my hand rather roughly then hauled me up into sitting position and put an arm around my shoulders.

"You and me, we're all right aren't we, Boyzie?"

I did not pull away, but I shivered involuntarily as he held my body tightly against his own. What kind of a relationship did the bloke want with me? I knew exactly what kind of relationship I wanted with him; the kind of one mate with another. Two blokes who got along well together, enjoyed some of the same pursuits like watching football, going out for a few jars, eating a good meal together, sharing lewd jokes, as and when the time was right, and gaining solace and comfort from one another's company when necessary. I wanted to enjoy a good chat, watch television together or go out to the pictures or somewhere like that from time to time, drive around together, even read books or magazines together. Andy often read to me from the paper, magazines or the Sunday papers when we were alone. It was obvious he appeared to want something more! A closer and more profound relationship! Perhaps I was wrong! Oh God, I hoped so, because I really did not want that kind of relationship, neither with him, nor with any other bloke.

We still sat together on my bed, Andy with his arm around my shoulders and his body pressed hard up against mine.

"Cum on, mate! Let's be friends again, eh?"

He moved closer to me, if indeed that was possible, so that he was almost on top of me, and pushed me down onto the bed so we were lying pressed tight up together, side by side on our backs, our legs stretched out in front of us. Andy still had a protective arm clamped around me. I felt hot all over and distinctly uncomfortable as we lay there, our bodies pressed tightly together!

"I didn't mean to hurt you, Boyzie! I'm… I'm very fond of you, mate! You know that don't you?"

I could not speak! My eyes were brimming with unshed tears and I still felt angry with him. I felt angry, hot, frustrated, violated, used and betrayed, and now I was being asked just to forget about everything that had transpired and forgive him for his outburst and his behaviour towards me. No, I did not think I could do it!

"Please!" Andy was saying. "Please forgive me, Boyzie, and let's start again eh? Cum on, mate. You know you want to!"

He drew me towards him and once more endeavoured to squeeze me breathless in a massive bear hug. I gasped, and now I did struggle, and managed to pull myself away.

"Please, Andy, I don't want this! I don't want this kind of relationship with you!" I was now on my feet, standing on the right-hand side of the bed. "I'm hot. I'm going to have a shower. When I've done, we'll sit down together and have dinner. How's that sound?" I asked, and I walked out of the bedroom and into the bathroom to undertake the procedure to which I had just referred.

"Bollocks, Boyzie!" he roared. "I've got dinner ready an' nah aw'm gonna sit an' 'av my meal, an' a drink or two, an' you can go to blazes!"

He was shouting, banging and crashing about the flat as I was engaged in having my shower. My head was aching and I felt rotten. Was it only a short while before that I had felt so good, having learned that I had been successful in obtaining the position of trainee counsellor at the Family Support Centre? My new 'mate', Andy, had succeeded in spoiling all that for me.

I stood under the shower, letting the warm water cascade down all around me and upon me. It was pleasant, it was soothing, but I was soon abruptly and rudely interrupted again. I did not hear his approach! I was lathering myself with soap under the gentle spray of water when I suddenly felt the heat and the pressure being turned up.

"*Andy!*" I shouted.

I heard him laugh drunkenly.

"Thought you might need a bit o' cooling dahn, Boyzie!" he yelled, and now the water was coming down on me in torrents, and it was freezing cold.

Shivering, I made attempts to climb out of the shower, but he pushed me back in! He turned off the water and climbed in with me, completely naked! He pushed me backwards, so that I fell and hit my head. He straddled me as I lay on my back in the shower. He was heaving himself up and down, up and down upon my body. He had a hand clamped over my mouth, and I was having difficulty breathing. I was absolutely terrified! My whole body was frozen, as though in a profound state of shock. My head was singing, and the pain was throbbing through it where it had struck the floor of the shower unit.

Andy was still sprawled on top of me. He was singing, singing drunkenly. I discovered later that he had downed a whole bottle of rough cider and half another one, and was stoned out of his head! He was writhing on top of me, and his hands were all over me. He was grunting, groaning, swearing, singing, heaving himself up and down upon me then suddenly, he came. He came all over me and as he did so he roared out obscenities and once more began to sing at the top of his voice.

"Here we go, here we go, here we go! Here we go, here we go, here we go-oh!"

I felt sick! I could feel my stomach heaving. I lay there, as if dead, while he came all over me a second time. He heaved his body off mine and stood over me. He pointed his penis downwards and urinated all over me as I lay almost senseless on the floor of the shower unit. With both feet he commenced kicking me then he was on his hands and knees, pummelling me with both fists and kicking me with his large bare feet! As he did so, he was roaring out:

"Aw luv yo', aw luv yo', yo' bastard!"

I think I must have blacked out then!

෫෨෴෫

The first thing I noted as I came to was the terrible smell! It seemed to be emanating from me and from the area all around me, then I realised how cold I felt, and struggled to sit up. Oh! Oh my good God! My head felt twice, no, three times its original size. The pain searing through my head, no, through my whole body, was indescribable.

I lay back for a few moments, resting my aching head against the wall of the shower unit. Things were slowly coming into perspective. I began to really remember what had happened since I had arrived home at God only knew what time it was, and whoever knew what time it was now? I lay still on the floor in the shower unit, slowly realising exactly where I was. I sprawled on the dirty floor and rested my head, which was splitting. I believed that if I lifted it again it might very well unhinge itself and come away from its moorings! I could not stay there indefinitely. No, I had to move, I had to get myself up onto my feet, somehow or other, and clean up the mess in there. I had to wash, no, *scrub* my whole body from top to toe, several times, if necessary. I had to clean my teeth, again and again, as my mouth felt like the bottom of a parrot's cage, and try to figure out what I should do. Those decisions could wait for now, as just getting onto my feet would constitute a major difficulty.

I lay still, listening. All appeared silent within the flat. Was he in, or was he out with his mates getting even more drunk? If so, what could I expect when he arrived back at the flat later on that night? Oh my good God, I was thinking like a battered wife! I could not, I *would* not stay there and be treated like that. As I lay there, the pain searing through my head, I thanked someone up there that my brother, Eric, had advised me to keep the tenancy of the house in Milling Street. At least, if I had to do so, I could move back there and away from harm. To stay where I was would mean I was in imminent danger from someone who wished me great damage. I groaned inwardly, and the sound escaped from me almost unwittingly.

Afterwards, I lay listening again in my current abode, sprawled on the dirty floor of the shower unit. No! No sound was audible from anywhere in the flat, so perhaps I ought to try and get myself sorted out, and maybe I could either get into bed or else get away from there before he returned. My head was aching so badly. Ooh! I really wanted to go to bed and just sleep it off, but I knew I had to get out of there. Yes, I had to go, it would be folly to stay there and take another battering from him when he arrived back later on, perhaps in the company of an army of his drunken mates, who might wade in and help him to finish me off. Oh Christ!

With a supreme effort I managed to raise my body from the

floor and then, by easy movements, I was able to stagger to my feet and get my balance. I was still naked and very cold. I reached a hand out and found a big towel, which I wrapped around myself. I gingerly stepped out of the shower unit and steadily, slowly, made my way around the flat. Yes! I was alone, entirely alone! He must have gone out after he had done what he had done to me. The bastard! The lousy stinking bastard! Well, I would bathe, dress, pack my bags and arrange for a taxi. I would ring Bob's Cabs and get Bob Douse to come over and fetch me. He could take me back to Milling Street, and I would have to sleep on the put-you-up sofa in the front room that night. I had to get on with it, or else it would be too late. He would be home and then God only knew what might transpire!

Slowly, carefully, I went back into my bedsit, the only room into which I had not been since I left the shower unit. I found him spark out on the floor at the bottom of my bed. Beside him was an empty cider bottle and – oh, my good God - an empty bottle that had at one time contained paracetamol! How did I know it had contained paracetamol? He had taken it from my bedside table. The bottle had been three-quarters full of pills the evening before when I had taken two because I had had a bit of a headache. I guess I had been thinking of the following day and my forthcoming interview. Oh, how long ago all that seemed. If my calculations were correct, he must have taken an inordinately large number of pills, and how much had he had to drink? I knew he had consumed at least a bottle and a half of rough cider prior to his battering of me in the shower. Now there was another empty cider bottle on the floor of my bedsit, and how many more were there in the flat?

Why are you even thinking like this, Boyzie? Don't you know that time is passing by, and on the floor in this room is sprawled the body of a bloke you used to call your mate? He might be dead, and you are just standing here, a towel around your feet, wondering how much cider he has consumed prior to taking how ever many pills he has swallowed. Come on, mate! Pull yourself together and take some action - some positive action to help him before... before... Why should I help him? Why the jocking hell should I? He had abused me. He had used me and dealt with me disgracefully. He had battered me, punching and kicking me all around the floor of the shower unit, and cracking my head on the floor and against the wall until I had begged for mercy. He had straddled me and laughed like a maniac! He had come all over me at least twice to my certain knowledge, and then... then he had stood over me and... and... No! I did not feel inclined to help him in any way, even though I knew what state he was in, how much he had had to drink and the number of pills he must have taken. I did not feel inclined to...

I suddenly heard it - the knock on the front door of the flat. Oh hell! Who on earth could that be, calling on us at that time of the evening? The knocking came again, more urgently that time. I steeled myself, wrapped the big towel even more tightly around my naked body and went to the door to see who was outside awaiting admittance to the chaos within.

"Hello Boyzie!"

It was Steven Mannion and his flatmate, Colin Pilcher, who lived at Flat One, just across the wide hallway from ours. They were our immediate neighbours on the ground floor.

"Andy invited us to cum over this evenin' and 'av a drink wiv yo', mate!" said Colin, in his deep, resonant voice with its rich, North Midland accent.

I shook and shivered all over! Both men saw my reaction, and Steve Mannion, the younger of the two, looked past me into the flat.

"Is everyfink all reet, Boyzie?" he asked.

I was shaking! Shaking with cold and with fear! Both blokes moved over to me and Colin put a comforting and steadying arm around my shoulders.

"Wot's bin goin' on 'ere, Boyzie?" he asked, as Steve pushed past me and walked into the utter chaos that was spread around the main living area.

"Aw Christ!" he shouted. "It looks like World War Three has started!"

I was leaning helplessly against Colin, who now held me up with both arms around me.

"In the bedsit on the right," I moaned.

Colin helped me inside and closed the door behind him as Steve walked into my bedsit.

"Oh! Oh my lord!" he said, standing stock still in the doorway of the room. "Colin! Sit 'im dahn, an' get the kettle on! Aw'm gonna phone f'er an amblance!"

10

I WAS SITTING in the foyer of the County Hospital, with Andy Bold, Joe Capper and Father Martyn beside me.

We are awaiting news of Andy. They had rushed him into the emergency room then into the theatre, where he was still stretched out as they pumped his stomach to relieve him of the booze and other contents that he had swallowed back at the flat on that horrible night. I was very tired, but all the tiredness had evaporated from me. Now I just felt a sense of dread, a sense of horror for the future. What if… what if? I steeled myself not to think about that possibility. No! No, I mustn't! Not someone else in my life leaving me. No! Not again, not so soon after the late Paul McGowan had left me. Surely Andy would pull through, and yet, as I sat there with the other blokes all sitting around me unsure of what to say to me, I was pondering on why I should care.

He had battered me! He had abused me and used me frightfully the previous night, yet there I was, sitting in the foyer at the County Hospital, worrying about whether or not he would survive! I ought not to care. No! I ought not to care a damn as to whether the bastard survived. He had hurt me dreadfully, and I could not forget that, or the way he had abused my body with kicks and punches, and the vile behaviour that had taken place as he sprawled upon me when I was lying flat out on the floor of the shower unit at the flat. No! I ought not to care a damn about whether or not he survived, but I did. Oh yes, I did. I didn't want him to die without us having at least tried to make our peace! He had been a good mate to me during most of the time we had known one another, so I did not want us to part in that way. No! No! I did not want that to be the end of our relationship!

A procession of members of his family had been to see him that night, at least they had all come into the hospital with the intention of seeing him. Only his mother and Father Martyn had been allowed to be with him, and then only for a very short space of time. Father Martyn had intended to administer the last rites as they were a Catholic family, but apparently Andy was now an agnostic, so Father had waived the rites and was just there because I was.

⋛⋗⋖⋚

Martyn and the two policemen, Joe Capper and Andy Bold, had all arrived at the flat with a number of other people for a drinking party to which Andy had apparently invited them all the previous night! I had been taken back to the bathroom by Colin after Steve rang for the ambulance, and he had run a bath for me and had helped me into it. I had just sat there, so he and Steve stayed around and gave me what assistance they could while others who had just arrived saw Andy placed onto a stretcher then, together with two medics and the driver, and flanked by the crowd of friends, he was royally escorted to the waiting ambulance that apparently arrived very promptly to take him to the hospital. After Andy had gone, along with Jane Bonnier and Father Martyn in attendance, others present endeavoured to clear up the flat and make the place habitable again.

I had been asked to explain what had transpired, and was then asked if I wished to bring charges against Andrew David Gange for his treatment of me. I was too tired to think, so they told me to try and get some rest and let them know in the morning, when several police personnel would pay me a visit at the flat! I had not been able to rest! The flat was full of people assessing the situation, considering everything from all angles, talking, talking, talking, and I just wanted peace! My head still ached abominably, and I was given paracetamol for it and also a sedative to help me relax.

Soon after midnight the phone had rung and Jane Bonnier from the hospital had imparted information to those waiting at the flat as to how things were progressing with regard to Andy. I had managed to snatch a couple of hours sleep after the sedative was administered, and was very drowsy when I awoke, but equally determined that I would go to the hospital to see how he was faring. Thus, Joe Capper and Andy Bold, who are both good mates of Andy, together with Colin and Steve, who had hardly left my side since their arrival at the flat and who sat together with me in the back of Joe's car, drove me over to the hospital to see Andy.

⊱⊰

We were waiting to hear how he was doing and to know if and when I would be allowed to spend any time with him once he was back from theatre and reinstalled in the high dependency care unit. Time passed, and I was beginning to feel very tired! Joe, Andy Bold, Father Martyn and Steve and Colin, who were now back from getting drinks for everyone, were sitting around me and trying to talk to me to keep me awake and to buoy up my spirits - without a great deal of success! I was plunging into a slough of despondency.

⊱⊰

It was 4.25 a.m. on that long, seemingly never-ending Thursday morning! I had dozed fitfully as I sat waiting there in the foyer of the County Hospital, surrounded by those who cared about the condition of Andy, and also about me. Yes, I was still surrounded by friends. I was a lucky little beggar wasn't I though? I ought not to forget it either, but I felt so depressed that morning. I felt used, abused, humiliated and violated! Violated was not too strong a word for I *did* feel violated! He had violently and inten-

tionally abused me. He had masturbated on my body and then...
and then... Oh! Oh God! I couldn't bring myself to even think of
it because it hurt too much.

I was shaking again as I came awake, and felt someone gently
touch my shoulder.

"Boyzie!"

Several voices were speaking to me all at once, like the three
Williams brothers used to do in days gone by! Well, those days
were not so very far off! Oh yes they were, Boyzie! The years had
rolled onwards, and I had hardly ever thought of the Williams
brothers until then.

"Boyzie!" Father Martyn was saying. "The doctor says we can
go in and see him now, if you feel able to do so, Boyzie."

I was given encouragement by those who still sat around waiting for news, along with me, their mate! I was very grateful for
their presence, but I was most grateful to Father Martyn, and indeed to Steve Mannion and Colin Pilcher for the help they had
afforded me over the past few hours. I was helped to my feet, and
with Father Martyn's arm around my shoulders, and followed at a
short distance by my two stooges, Steve and Colin, I was escorted
to the doorway of Ward Eight on the ground floor of the hospital.
I was shown into the side room off the ward and allowed to sit in
a chair beside the bed in which he lay.

He was asleep, I was told, and I could hear his shallow breathing. He was lying on his back, and had two drips, one in each arm.
His right hand was on top of the counterpane as I sat next to the
bed. I reached out gingerly and touched it!

"Andy," I breathed, "oh, Andy!"

I was suddenly engulfed by a flood of helpless tears that simply
flowed from my eyes and completely overwhelmed me. I sat there
for a while like that, with Martyn sitting close beside me, his arm
draped protectively around my shaking shoulders. Suddenly there
was a movement in the bed. Andy appeared to rally for a few moments, and as he did so, I guess recognition must have dawned
upon him.

"Hello Oyshie!" he said, in what sounded like a drunken slur. "Aw'm sorry, mate, so sorry, Oyshie!"

I had not expected to hear his voice, even if his speech sounded slurred, and he could not properly pronounce my nickname, and the fact that I had heard him actually talking to me stemmed the flow of tears, albeit briefly. I sat very still then put out my hand and touched his as it lay on top of the bed.

"Come on, you little fighter! You know you can do it! I'll... I'll help you all I can. I'll help you every step of the way, Andy. You and me together! There's nothing we couldn't achieve mate. Come on! Keep fighting, Andy, I know you can make it if you try. You and me! You and me together, we're gonna climb to the top of Mount Kilimanjaro!"

I chatted on in this inane fashion for a while before I realised he was fast asleep again.

"Come on, Boyzie! That's enough now, isn't it?" said Father Martyn, once more assisting me to my feet and placing a consoling arm around my shoulders to guide me back to the waiting area where the others would want to know what had been happening.

By then I had hold of Andy's hand as it lay on the bed, and I did not want to let go! Eventually, and somewhat reluctantly, I did leave him, and returned with Martyn to where the others were waiting for news. I was given a hot drink as I sat down, and Martyn related to the waiting audience what had transpired while we had been with Andy. As we sat talking and taking in what had occurred over the past few hours, two doctors came to talk to us. The two young doctors introduced themselves to me and Father Martyn. One was male, one female, and they were both foreign. The young male doctor introduced himself as Doctor Abdullah and the young and very attractive Asian female introduced herself, initially to Father Martyn only, as Doctor Suri Patel. Both spoke impeccable English, although Doctor Suri Patel had a very noticeable accent.

"We are endeavouring to stabilise your friend, Mr Boyzie, and we hope he will soon feel much better," said Doctor Abdullah.

"I'm called Mr Dickson," I corrected him. "My nickname is Boyzie."

Both doctors smiled. "You have many friends with you tonight, Boyzie," said Doctor Suri Patel. "You are a very lucky man, don't you know."

Yes! Yes, I did know!

"You have been to see him, I believe?" asked Doctor Abdullah.

"Yes!" Father Martyn responded on my behalf.

"He... he spoke to me," I volunteered, still very shaky.

"Aw, that's very good!" exclaimed Suri Patel with real interest and sincerity. "You must be delighted!"

I agreed that I was very pleased to hear him speak, but asked for a prognosis from the two very pleasant and friendly practitioners.

"We can't tell you that for certain. Not yet, Mr Boyzie... I mean, *Dickson!*" said Doctor Suri.

"No!" agreed Doctor Abdullah. "At present it's too close to call, but he appears to be making quite good progress. Keep hopeful, eh?"

He placed a hand on my right shoulder before both doctors departed to continue their shift work in the vast and extremely busy hospital in the early hours of that seemingly never-ending April morning!

§❧§

Time passed. I had been dozing again and it was 5 a.m. The hum of voices and the shuffling of many feet all around me awakened me once more to what was going on.

Andy's mom was now sitting beside me.

"Oh, my luv!" she said "Yo' mus' be so tired, sittin' 'ere all this toime, waitin' fr news! Yo' mus' really care abaht 'im! Ay, an' look at the way 'e used yo', an' still yo' stay arrahnd to see 'ow 'e is. Well! Aw tell yo' luv, if wot I 'ear is right, then 'e dun't deserve your loyalty, Boyzie! Naw! Naw 'e dun't, my luv!"

I had always got on well with Dorothy Gange, 'Little Dot' as everyone in the family called her, with great affection I should add!

"I... I know he treated me badly, but... well... I can't just rub him out of my life! Andy has been good to me in the past, and... well... I don't forget people who are good to me."

"He's a bastard!" said his brother, Terry, and his brother, Lenny, agreed. "He ought ter be shot f'r wot 'e done ter yo', mate!"

One of his sisters, I wasn't sure if it was Shirley or Carol, started to cry, and Bernie, the eldest of his four brothers, walked off with his arm around her to console her. The family was arriving en masse and most of his friends had gone by then. Only Father Martyn, Steve, Colin and I remained, sitting together in the midst of the large family circle in the foyer of the County Hospital.

Little Dot had been right! I was extremely tired, but I did not want to go. I hoped in my secret heart that they might let me go in and see him again, just once more before I left the hospital and went home. Home! Where was that? I could not go back to Depot Street, not that I wished to do so without Andy. I could not properly understand my feelings towards him at that moment. Even after he had used and abused me so violently, it seemed I still cared for him! It was only that, wasn't it, nothing more? No! No, nothing more, nothing sinister, just a very great 'fellow' feeling for one bloke to another, or was I kidding myself? Oh, I was far too tired to get myself into anything heavy at that early hour. It felt as though I had never been to bed that year! My head was dropping onto my chest, and my eyes were hurting with the effort of trying to stay awake and alert. Oh God, would that dreadful morning never reach its conclusion?

More coffee, more people coming and going, more chatter. More recriminations and observations, more shuffling and scuffling of feet!

§≈§

I slept fitfully through all that was going on around me, until eventually, at around 8.20 a.m., Father Martyn helped me to my feet.

"We can go in and say cheerio to him before I take you back to my place, Boyzie!"

"Is he still okay?" I asked querulously.

"Yes! Yes, he's holding his own well apparently! That's why we're being allowed in to see him again. Come on now, mate, and then I'm taking you home and helping you to bed. I bet you are hungry, yeh?"

Actually, the last thing on my mind was eating, but I was terribly thirsty. I was bone-weary! We walked together, arms around one another's shoulders, into the side room situated off Ward Eight, and once more, I was helped to seat myself on the chair beside the bed in which he still lay, sprawled on his back, a heart monitor and two drips still attached to him! Andy spoke.

"Hi Boyzie!" His speech sounded clearer now. "How goes it then, my owd mate?"

I did not know how to respond.

"I'm glad you seem a bit better, Andy," I volunteered, then suddenly felt choked, and I could hardly breathe!

Father Martyn quickly led me from the room as Andy called out, almost cheerfully, after us:

"See you later eh, Boyzie? Eh, Father?"

Martyn escorted me to his car, talking to me all the time. He settled me in the front seat and helped me to fasten my seat belt before wrapping a thick blanket around my legs. I was shaking! He realised I was probably in shock. He should perhaps have had some guidance from those at the hospital, perhaps from someone in the casualty unit, but he did not bother with any of that! Instead, he drove me back to Saint Jude's Convent, and helped me inside. There the Sisters, bless their warm hearts, waited upon both of us with great kindness and generosity of spirit. Sister Bridget, Sister Ruth, Sister Martha and Sister Rose Margaret waited upon both of us!

I was given a hot drink, and Sister Bridget sat beside me while I drank heartily, and talked quietly to me to calm me down. She was a lovely woman, in her mid to late forties, very Irish, with a lovely soothing lilt to her quiet, but strong, voice.

"Now then, just you sit here and relax, Boyzie. You are safe here. Nothing and no one can hurt you here, so just relax! Take your ease. Drink your tea, and then I'll get you another one and prepare a breakfast for you fit to give a king on his throne! There now, that's better, isn't it, luv?"

The lovely, kind, thoroughly enchanting Sisters of the Convent of Saint Jude!

෧**෧

Later, Father Martyn drove me back to the presbytery, where he helped me into bed and made me comfortable. Steve Mannion and Colin, his flatmate, had returned to Depot Street, but arrived later at the presbytery with two big holdalls full of things I might, or might not, require for a few days' stay with the priests; Father Martyn, Father Bernard and Father Dominic, and also the new novice who had recently arrived, one Brother Louis Sebastian.

Steve and Colin had a chat with Father Martyn and Father Dominic before coming into the room where it had been arranged that I would stay during my sojourn there. They fetched in the two bulging holdalls, plus four or five large carrier bags full of belongings from our flat, which they had taken from my bedsit with my permission. They told me they would leave the bags for me to sort out when I got up and felt better. Both men sat with me for a while before the door was opened and the young novice, Brother Louis Sebastian, brought a tray of tea and scrambled eggs on toast for me.

"The Fathers say try and eat something if you are able please, Boyzie!" said the young man anxiously as he placed the tray on the bed before me.

Encouraged by him, plus Steve and Colin, who stayed a little longer, I endeavoured to do justice to the meal that had been prepared for me. I could eat nothing at the Convent of Saint Jude and I was not able to eat anything then, despite trying! I was feeling extremely emotional, my throat was hurting, my head was splitting and I was finding it difficult to swallow without feeling considerable pain. However, I had had several drinks whilst at the convent and since I had been taken to the presbytery, and had thoroughly relaxed in the presence of the good and kind Sisters. I had talked with Sister Bridget, Sister Winifred and Mother Mary Magdalene. Mother was a very gracious woman, only in her mid-thirties, but she was so kind and understanding.

"You may remain here or at the presbytery for as long as you require to do so, Boyzie," she told me. "We know you are not of our faith, but we are glad to be able to help you nonetheless, and you must avail yourself of our comforts and our company while these are required."

"Thanks, Mother. You are very kind," I rejoined, but I had been so very, very tired, I hardly knew what I was saying.

As I lay back against the pillows piled behind me, in the room with the windows wide open so the warm spring air could pervade, with no one to bother me, although people were near if I required assistance, I could endeavour to sleep. When I awoke I would be able to think. To think more rationally and perhaps discuss my situation with others in a calmer, more sensible manner.

I put aside the tray, having given up the struggle to eat any of the food that had been prepared for me by the kind, thoughtful Fathers at the Presbytery of Saint Jude, swallowed down half a mug of hot, sweet tea, then lay back, sprawled on my back in a nice, warm clean bed, with the windows of the room wide open to the elements and the sun shining in my eyes, but kindly, softly! I slept the sleep of the just!

11

I T WAS the early hours of Friday morning before I awoke! I lay for a while, trying to rally my thoughts and remember where I was. Suddenly, like a tide, it all came rushing over me once more. I needed to go to the bathroom, but of course I had no concept of where it was located. I moved in the bed, propping myself up on my right elbow then heaving myself up properly and throwing back the bedclothes that had been covering me.

In the other bed in the room, the young novice, Brother Louis Sebastian, awoke.

"Are you all right, Boyzie?" he asked.

I was now standing beside the bed.

"Er... sorry... I need the bathroom," I told him.

Brother Louis Sebastian, a young man of Anglo-French origin, climbed from his bed and, in his pyjamas and bare feet, escorted me to the bathroom and waited outside until I had performed my ablutions to my satisfaction. I still craved a long hot bath, and would ask if I could have one later on that morning.

"All right?" asked Brother Louis as I came out of the bathroom feeling considerably refreshed.

"Oh yeh, I could do with a long drink and a bath!"

He laughed good-naturedly.

"I will help you back into your bed then I shall go downstairs to the kitchen and make for us an early breakfast. You have not yet eaten, no? I think you have not eaten for some time! I shall make for us an early breakfast and a hot drink. For me, a mug of coffee, for you, a large mug of hot chocolate! How's that sound eh, Boyzie?"

I said it sounded grand! Young Brother Louis Sebastian helped me back into bed, made sure I was comfortable then went off downstairs. He returned about half an hour later with a loaded tray. He had made us both a drink - coffee for him, the promised mug of hot chocolate for me. Also on the tray he carried was a large plate containing four, big crusty cobs full of bacon, smothered in red sauce!

"There! Eat up, Boyzie!" said the young novice.

We enjoyed our repast, sitting together side by side on the edge of my single bed. Louis Sebastian was a tall young man of Anglo-French descent. He was in his late teens, and was greatly looking forward to becoming a priest and working in the vast and busy parish of Saint Jude, there in Gaynsford. He said that Fathers Bernard, Dominic and Martyn were very kind to him and very accepting of all his mistakes, which he freely admitted were many at first, and that under their guidance he was beginning to settle into the new and demanding regime of the young novice's life. He would be pleased, he told me, to share his rooms with me for as long as I wished to remain there. It would be good to have someone else to talk with and with whom I could spend some time. I told him I hoped I would prove to be as good a companion as he believed I might, but that there was a lot for me to think about at that time, so if at times I proved to be not quite as attentive as perhaps he would wish then I hoped he would forgive me!

"Certainly! I realise that your life is turned upside down at the moment, but we are all here to help you, Boyzie. You do know that, don't you, my friend?" he asked, and placed a comforting hand upon my right arm.

"Thanks Louis," I told him, and gave his big hand a squeeze.

He was a good lad, who loved sport, light classical and 'smooth' jazz music, long walks, 'real ale', playing darts and snooker, reading comics and murder mysteries, and visiting fairgrounds, among other pursuits! I suggested that he would fit in with the three rather lively Fathers who shared the presbytery very well indeed, and he laughed and said yes, that was certainly the case and he was very happy there.

At first he had missed his home environment, and he longed to return to Brittany, where his family lived, or at least where his parents lived, and also Normandy where other aunts, uncles and indeed two of his sisters were resident with their families.

"But you know, Boyzie, I believe this is where my life will be for a while to come. Here in the parish of Saint Jude! This is where I wish to stay from now on, and for some time in the future, learning all I am able from the Holy Fathers."

I smiled despite the weight of the worries piling in upon me. I liked that young man; he was honest, straightforward and friendly, and obviously very keen on the life he had chosen. I believed we would get on very well together for the time we would spend in each other's company.

After we had finished our early breakfast, we both crept out of the bedroom on bare feet and went downstairs to the kitchen. We washed the pots quietly then returned upstairs to the bedroom. We were whispering like a couple of naughty schoolboys who were afraid they would be 'caught snacking', and we were both laughing fit to beat the band by the time we got back upstairs. I was feeling better than I had for some time. That young man was doing me a power of good.

Later, when I got back into bed again, I lay there thinking for ages, and my thoughts were not pleasant. They were of an uncertain future, for which I did not as yet feel entirely prepared. I knew that I would receive a good deal of help and support along the way. Once my family knew what had happened, then they would… No! I quickly turned my thoughts away from that scenario! I did not want my family to discover what had occurred, and later that day, when I saw them, I would tell the Fathers that, and ensure that they were not informed. If Eric, my brother, had any inkling of what had taken place, there would be all hell to pay, I was certain of that, so at that stage anyway, it would be better if the family 'down south' did not know anything about what had gone on over the past couple of days. Yes, that was definitely the best solution. 'Keep it dark, eh,' as my lovely late and still lamented Grannie Annie would have put it. 'Keep it dark!' I finally drifted off into slumber again.

ૄౢﾰﾊ

When I awoke once more it was well after 8 a.m. and I was alone in the room. The four priests must be up and were either at prayers or else they might have been together in the study, or in the refectory.

I lay in bed for a while, savouring the warmth and the fact that I felt so much better. As I lay still on my back in the warm comfortable bed, I heard the phone ringing away in the hallway down below. After a few moments I heard footsteps then a discussion outside the bedroom door before a hand knocked and the door was opened about an inch.

"Boyzie!" called Father Martyn's voice. "Is it okay for us to come in?"

"Sure," I called back cheerfully.

The door was flung open wide, and Martyn, Dominic and young Louis Sebastian walked into the room together. I sat up in the bed and they sat in a row along it! After a few moments, we were joined by Father Bernard, who deposited his ample frame in the armchair at the side of the bed on the right. He spoke first, breaking the somewhat uneasy silence in the room.

"Boyzie! How are you feeling now?"

"Much better," I told him and the others present, "but I could do with a long drink!"

Brother Louis was dispatched to the kitchen to fulfil my request. The others stayed with me, all sitting around the bed. We talked quietly together until Brother Louis Sebastian returned with a mug of hot tea for me.

"Now then, Boyzie!" said Father Bernard. "We have had some news from the hospital, and it's not good I am afraid."

I stopped, the mug halfway to my mouth.

"Oh! What's happened? Please tell me what's h-happened," I insisted, my voice beginning to tremble, my hands beginning to shake.

Father Martyn put his arm around my shaking shoulders while Brother Louis relieved me of the half-full mug of hot sweet tea. Father Bernard moved over in the chair and took my right hand in his.

"Andy was very comfortable last night, Boyzie, but early this morning, at about 5 a.m., he suffered a massive brain haemorrhage…"

I did not hear the rest of what Father Bernard was telling me. All I could 'see' in my confusion, in the eye of my befuddled mind, was Andy, lying in that bed beside which I had sat the day before in the early hours of the morning. All I could hear was his voice in my head, the slurring of his words as he had said, speaking with difficulty:

"*Aw'm sorry! So sorry, Oyshie!*"

I would not cry. No! No, I would not cry. I had to be strong. That was what he would expect of me. Now I had to be strong for both of us. I could see him in my mind's eye, sitting with me on the couch at the flat in Depot Street, reading the newspaper on the morning of the day last week - when I had gone for my interview - was it really only last week?

"*Hey-up, Boyzie! You know any of these blokes?*"

He had read out the three names, Philip Mackie, Graham Roddis, Steven Gregson.

"*Well, they are certainly aiming high!*" he had exclaimed, before continuing. "*They are all blind, and they are determined to climb to the summit of Mount Kilimanjaro!*"

Yes! As I sat there listening to the chatter taking place among the four young priests assembled with me in that big airy bedroom in the presbytery of Saint Jude, I was determined that we too, me and Andy Gange, would climb our own mountain, and was equally determined that, all things considered, we'd reach the bloody summit together as well! As my mind came back into focus, my ears once more were attuned to the intonation of Father Bernard's voice.

"He's still alive, but he's in the high dependency unit and is on a life support system."

No! Oh no! Whatever happened Andy must not die! He must not leave me! I couldn't cope with anyone else leaving me at that moment. Was I being utterly selfish? No! No, I wasn't, but I could not and would not let him die! If there was any way I could prevent it then I would. Stupid thoughts were chasing one another through my confused aching head, and Father Bernard's voice was droning on. I shut my mind and my ears to what was being said, and lay back on the pillows piled behind me with my eyes tightly shut, as though I did not want to hear any more.

Eventually, Father Bernie let go of my hand and he and young Father Dominic rose to their feet. They abruptly left the room together, talking quietly. Martyn and the ever loyal Brother Louis Sebastian remained with me, sitting one on each side of the bed, each holding on to one of my trembling hands! We sat like that for some considerable time. Both men talked quietly and easily to me as we sat there together, but I still would not cry. All kinds of thoughts were tumbling through my pounding head!

I was in bed at the presbytery for four days following the revelation that Andy had suffered a brain haemorrhage. The shock was very, very great! I had dared to believe, when I last sat beside the bed in which he lay in the small room situated off Ward Eight in the County Hospital, that maybe he was going to make it and that he would soon be allowed home. The two doctors, Doctor Abdullah and Doctor Suri Patel, had given me to understand that, despite problems, his progress was satisfactory. No, that was wrong! They had stated within my hearing and that of Father Martyn that Andy's progress to date was more than satisfactory. They had also said that, although they were unable to give me a complete prognosis of his situation, they were fairly sure that he would pull through. Now, there was Father Bernard telling me that in the early hours of the morning, on Friday, 20 April 1990, Andy had suffered that major blow - a blow that was life-threatening and that had resulted in his being placed on a life support system in the high dependency care unit!

The news was totally devastating. Again, as thoughts tumbled one after another through my confused mind, I upbraided myself for even daring to care! Why should I care whether or not he lived or died after everything he had done to me? You see, I had known a very different Andy from the one who had so vilely and cruelly used and abused me a few nights before. The bloke I had known was warm, caring, understanding, friendly, amusing, liked long walks, rock music, good food, parties and his work at the police headquarters in Bread Street, Allerton! He had enjoyed living with me, learning about me and the way in which I lived my life, also learning that, despite my being almost devoid of vision apart from perception of light, I was nevertheless very capable of living an extremely full and active life. Indeed, I had performed many duties around the flat in order to support him while he was out at work. In effect, I had been what they call nowadays a 'house husband', undertaking duties such as preparation of meals and hot drinks, making the beds, dusting around, washing his socks, shirts and a mountain of other clothing, keeping the place tidy etc., etc.

When one has a visual disability or deficiency, it is necessary - more necessary than when one has one's full degree of sight - to endeavour to be as tidy and as organised as possible in one's domestic arrangements. If this were not so, particularly in my own case, I would have grave problems in so far as I would have little or no idea of where anything was, and thus, my life could become fraught with risks and subsequent danger. Even making a hot drink can become full of difficulties if one has a lack of vision! Andy had learned very quickly how to help me and how to ensure that he and I lived amicably together in the flat we shared in the town centre opposite the car park. Could we ever return there and be together again? I did not imagine so. No, I could not ever envisage that he would ever be able to come home, and certainly, if he did, then I could see no way that he and I could ever live together in that accommodation again.

I reasoned dully as I lay there in the warm bed in my shared room at the presbytery of Saint Jude. Why would I wish to share a flat with him again after the abominable way in which he had treated me the previous Wednesday night? I still cared for him! Yes, I still… Oh! Go on, Boyzie, admit it to yourself if to no one else! You love the guy! No! No point in beating about the bush. What you feel for Andrew David Gange is plain and simple love, nothing more, nothing less! Plain, simple, honest-to-goodness love! The love and respect for one bloke to another, or was it perhaps something more tangible? No! I had never possessed those kind of feelings for any other bloke.

Granted, I had lots of mates and, of course, I had deep-rooted feelings for many of them, and for neighbours who had lived in the Circle and in Rutland Close, where I had lived previously. Also for guys I worked with or knocked around with, blokes who drove me around the town and gave me assistance during the course of my daily life, and the 'network' of young people that had wrapped itself around me and afforded me such invaluable assistance throughout a period of many years! For people now gone; my mate, Rob McCallasky and the late Paul McGowan, whom, although we only knew each other for a brief time while we were both domiciled in the County Hospital, had a profound effect upon my life. For the priests who were now affording me such excellent care and endeavouring to sustain me throughout the difficult time through which I was currently living and, of course, for my mate, Andy!

No matter what he had done to me in the recent past, he had been my mate, I still cared for him very deeply, and I cared about what happened to him and how he would survive and cope, with or without support, in the future! Naïve? Yeh, perhaps I was, but then I always had been 'soft', I knew that from past experiences and past relationships. A person can't help his or her make-up. I guess a lot of it stems from when I was away at boarding school between the ages of four and 18 years - the vast majority of my childhood spent away from my family and among virtual strangers. I used to hate it when I had to leave home or people, or even when anyone had to leave me! I used not to try and build ongoing relationships because I knew that eventually those would have to end. When they did, I used to become very emotional, and that still applies, even to this day!

A person can learn from his or her mistakes when involved in relationships, or at least he or she should learn to do this, but somehow I never seemed to manage to do so, not until I was hurt, which was then too late, of course! By then the damage had been done!

With such thoughts tumbling around in my head, I drifted off into a troubled slumber, during which I had many strange dreams, and tossed and turned a great deal. In the course of those troubled dreams I saw many characters from my past life. I saw Susan! She was running along a wide street, her hair flying out behind her in the wind. As she ran, she was calling out to me, but the wind was carrying the words she was saying away from me, and I could not properly hear what she said. I saw my Grannie Annie and my Uncle Sid. Sid was then married to Brenda and they lived in Portsworth in Hampshire, where Brenda ran a shop and Sid still drove taxis with his mate, Ernie, whom he had met in the navy.

I saw Rob McCallasky as he had been on the day of the terrible tragedy that had taken place in Glosport. He had been all fired up, eager and enthusiastic for the game to be played that day between Glosport and our glorious team, Gaynsford United, the League and First Division Champions! I saw Eric learning about what had recently transpired with regard to me at the flat in Depot Street and I perceived, in the course of my dream, how very angry and upset he was about Andy's behaviour towards me! I saw Johnnie Friscoe as she had been on the first wonderful evening that she and I had spent together when we met while I was staying with Yvonne and Eric in Cherry Wootton. I saw Maura O'Reilly and also Honey Laverne!

I saw Marjorie McNault on the day when she rescued me from the crowds of lads who had pushed me into the middle of the road in front of a truck, and I saw her daughter, Alice May, who had been so kind and loving towards me on that fateful day! I saw Johnnie again, when she stabbed me with the knife on New Year's Day 1990. I saw Les Greaves scoring the winning goal against Glosport when we won the League Cup in 1978, and Johnnie and I racing around the track at Brawnstone, Northamptonshire, on that magic day back in August of the same year.

Everything was so strange! All those dreams and situations were running into one another, and I could not tell where one began and another ended. It was all very frightening.

§⇒❧§

In the early hours of Saturday morning, the Fathers called a doctor to me because they believed I was feverish. Doctor Kathleen Moss, a woman with a rather deep, smooth husky voice and a pleasant easy manner, came to my bedside and took my left hand. She took my pulse, felt my forehead and took my temperature.

"Is he drinking well?" I heard her ask.

"No!" answered a chorus of male voices.

"You must try and get him to drink of his own volition, or I'll have to have him hospitalised in order to prevent dehydration," said Doctor Moss quietly, but firmly, to the three priests and the young novice assembled around the bed in the large, warm and comfortable room that I currently shared with Brother Louis Sebastian.

"See if you can get him to drink something warm as soon as possible, and if he won't then try him with a little cool water. You must make sure he sips it though, don't let him gulp it down!"

She gave me two quite deep injections then she and Father Bernard propped me up in the bed and made me comfortable. There was a degree of discussion around the bed, but it droned through my head as I was now beginning to feel very drowsy. That

77

was the injections taking hold. Soon I was in a very deep sleep, and I slept on and off for the next three and a half days!

12

IT WAS a week into the new school year. In three different locations, in three very diverse schools, the same event was taking place during school assembly, and the local media were lapping it up!

At Saint Cecilia's Roman Catholic Primary School on Clarke Street in Whatton, a large and expanding town in East Anglia, Graham Roddis and his guide dog, Ted, the head teacher, all the teaching staff and approximately 450 young people had assembled in the main hall. At the Trent Community and Sports College on Trent Street, Allendale, an industrial town in the East Midlands, Steven Gregson was with his new guide dog, Jason, a large and very lively German shepherd, recently qualified. They were in the gymnasium of the college, in front of about 1,000 students and all the Years Seven, Eight and Nine teaching staff. There were also members of the local press present at both establishments, waiting for what was to come!

Down in the city of Greymarsh in Essex, at Castle Hill Community Primary School, Castle Hill, Philip Mackie, who was not a guide dog owner, was domiciled in the large and brand new building known as Valentine House, which had been paid for from the legacy of the late Councillor Norman Valentine. He had been a pupil at the school and later a school governor for nigh on 30 years before his untimely decease, the result of an accident towards the end of the previous year. He had left instructions and the money for the building to be designed and built for the purpose of education at the establishment he had always greatly revered. Those in authority within that haven of education were most grateful to the good and esteemed Councillor Valentine for his patronage and his generosity, which had resulted in a brand new extension to their premises.

The entire school was assembled in the new assembly hall of Valentine House to await a very exciting and very special announcement that their visitor, Mr Philip Mackie, was about to make concerning his forthcoming adventure! He intended to make it at exactly, or as near as possible, the same time as his two colleagues in Allendale and Whatton - a simultaneous and momentous announcement that would hopefully enthuse and excite a great many people!

The schools mentioned above were the first of many that the three blind men, two of them with their guide dogs in tow, would be visiting over the coming weeks and months. The local journalists were craning their necks and straining their ears in order to learn what was going on, and there were photographers poised, ready to take the pictures that would accompany the articles in the local papers later on that day. After all, if three blind men intended to climb to the summit of Mount Kilimanjaro and endeavoured to raise more than £150,000 to help cure river blindness in Africa in the process – well, it was big news indeed, or at least their editors thought so!

13

Monday, 17 September 1990.

IT WAS a morning that had already succumbed to the feeling
that summer was over and autumn was coming in fast. The
trees were changing colour and the leaves were beginning to
drift down onto the ground. The summer sunshine and gentle
winds were replaced that morning with a much colder feel to the
weather, although it was still fine, even if it was a great deal cooler
than of late.

I was glad of it. The summer had been beautiful, but very hot
and sticky. Now the cooler weather was upon us perhaps things
would feel a little less oppressive, at least as far as the weather was
concerned. Heaven knew I had enough to oppress and depress me
at that moment, although having said that, I still had lots of support from family, friends and acquaintances.

After leaving the shelter and sanctuary of the presbytery of Saint
Jude's I had returned to my council house in Milling Street, feeling totally unable to go back to Depot Street without Andy. I was
visiting him almost daily in the convalescent unit at the College
Hospital, and I knew that he was hoping I might feel able to let
him go back to my place once he was discharged. At present, nobody was entirely sure when that would be. Doctor Mishra had
told me she was uncertain as to when his discharge date would be,
owing to the fact that before he could go home they would require
to ensure that he would be safe and able to function adequately in

his new home situation, whatever and wherever that might happen to be.

I had been quizzed by the staff at the College Hospital about having him to live with me, and I had considered that from a number of angles. From the point of view of the fact that if I did succumb and allow him to go home and live with me, I would of necessity have to have a number of alterations made to my house. Those would be quite sweeping, and would cost a good deal of money to undertake. Whilst that was not in itself a major problem, I sincerely wondered why the hell I should, or why I should even want to have all that work done so that I could have the arsehole living in my house! After everything he had recently put me through, did I really want to have him like a millstone around my neck for the rest of my life? Even as I thought like that, two other thoughts were uppermost in my confused mind. One was that it would not be for the rest of my life that I would have him with me. No! I knew from the conversations I had had with the medical staff that even if he came home from the convalescent unit, his time with me would not be long. The very severe brain haemorrhage that Andy had suffered had left him in a very weak and vulnerable condition.

Andy had worked hard to pull himself together, and had endeavoured to struggle back to full fitness. He had made extremely good progress. His speech had greatly improved, he could walk, although he did so with a rolling gait and became extremely tired very quickly, and his mood swings were improving vastly almost daily. He could wash, dress and feed himself, although sometimes it took a long time, and it always took a good deal of his strength to accomplish those daily tasks. He could manage to use the toilet virtually unaided, although he did sometimes need a little help with zips etc., especially when he felt very tired, and he had to wear pads and panties because at times he was still inclined to be incontinent. However, he was working hard to overcome all such problems, and was fighting fiercely to regain his independence. His eye, which had been working prior to that terrible tragedy, was functioning more adequately, but he was virtually having to learn to read and write once again as though he had never known how to do so. At times his speech was difficult to understand, especially when he became tired, then all his words tended to slur together and he became extremely frustrated and very unhappy. I could calm him! I was good for him! He loved me to visit, to be beside him as he sat in his wheelchair or reclined in one of the big chairs or on the sofa in his room, or else lay sprawled on the bed with me in the chair beside him. He loved me to be there with him, talking to him, holding his hand, making plans with him for 'our rosy future together'. When I had believed he was dying, I had commenced making those plans to myself, and had eventually started to relate them to him in the hope that by so doing I would help him to rally. Indeed, according to the medics, and by reason of the fact that I had witnessed it, that had eventually become a reality.

One day as I sat talking to the virtual corpse that lay sprawled on the bed beside which I was seated, as I had been for many days in the past, I was engaged in telling Andy how I would have him home to live with me once he was able to be discharged from the convalescent unit.

"I can help you to wash and to dress, mate, then afterwards I'll go along to the kitchen and get breakfast for both of us. You can choose what you want to eat and I'll prepare it for you, mate! When I come back, I'll help you to get into the chair where your table tray is and we'll eat breakfast together, with me helping you to feed yourself, Andy. Right? When we've finished breakfast and tidied around, and you've had a little rest, I'll shave, then I'll help you to shave, Andy, and later we might go down to the shops and maybe to the park. You'd like that, wouldn't you, mate? I can push you in your wheelchair, and you can have fun telling me, 'right here, Oyshie' and 'left here, Oyshie' etc., etc. That will be a laugh, won't it, eh?"

I had laughed then suddenly I had heard the sound of him beginning to laugh too. At first I did not believe it. Was I merely imagining what I was hearing, or what I believed I was hearing? No! The sound coming from the body lying on the bed was very real. It was the sound of laughter. I had broken through the barrier at last! From that day on, I kept talking to him, talking about the plans I was making for when he was released from hospital, released back to my care! It certainly looked as though that could become a reality.

᠖᠆᠖

I got up from my bed and went into the bathroom. I ran myself a bath and while the water was running into the tub I went downstairs to the kitchen and put the kettle on. Returning upstairs, I bathed, shaved, dressed and went down to have a cuppa before catching the bus to Allerton.

I was very much involved in the life of the counselling team based at the Family Support Centre on Bread Street, Allerton. I worked with Otis McKinley Masher, plus two other counsellors, one male, one female, and our team leader Pastor Jeremiah Johnson. Jeremiah Johnson was in his early forties, a big, tough, well-built, healthy-looking, strong-willed straightforward West Indian gentleman, always well dressed and clean-shaven, but with dreadlocks! Jeremiah Johnson, Pastor Jeremiah, was quite a character, and a well-respected man in the area. He was blunt, to the point, and did not suffer fools gladly! He was a devout believer, who was always very fair and listened to whatever one had to say. In truth, Jeremiah Johnson was a good boss, and I was happy working under him.

Mike Groves, the new director of the family support services in Gaynsford South, was a grand bloke, and his deputies, Shirley Beresford and Wayne Clarke, were both known to me. I was getting on well with my colleagues, and my job meant a great deal to me. The support I was receiving from all my friends and acquaintances was very great and very real, and I was, in truth, an extremely lucky bloke. I knew it, and I was grateful for it, but there was still a void in my life. Although in many ways I was fulfilled, there was still one major way in which I was not, and it irked me and left a big hole in my life. Despite everything I had, I was still desperately lonely, and longed for some permanent company, whether male or female! I just wanted someone to share my life, my thoughts, my time, my home, and I hoped he, or she, would come soon in order to save my sanity.

That was why I was so susceptible to the suggestion that I had Andy home to live with me. After all, at least he would be someone for me to care for, someone for whom I could clean, cook and wash, someone to whom I could talk, someone with whom I could plan, someone to whom I could read, someone with whom I could listen to music and with whom I could watch the TV etc. Yes! At least I would have someone in my life permanently, but did I necessarily want it to be him after all the lousy bastard had put me through? Did I need that jockin' millstone hanging around my neck?

Two thoughts pulled me up short, one being the fact that it would not be for long. Despite his unerring progress and the great efforts he had made in order to struggle to attain some semblance of normality, everyone knew, probably even Andy, that his recovery could never be complete. Indeed, I had learned from the medics that in all probability his life would be fairly short, and that he might live say for another five years, ten at most, but that was highly unlikely. Therefore, I ought to endeavour to ensure that his last years were happy years!

Secondly, and I had to be quite ruthless in order to make myself admit it, I knew in my secret heart that I still cared for Andy. Yes, as I had admitted to myself when I lay in bed in the room I had shared at the presbytery of Saint Jude, with the ever loyal Brother Louis Sebastian, now returned to Brittany to live and work, I loved Andy. Yes, I truly loved him and that was why I had to, of necessity, have him home to live with me on his imminent discharge from the convalescent unit. I was so very, very tired, and I knew my body was telling me it was time to slow down and relax. It was time for me to begin taking it easy, yet there I was, intending to take on an extra burden that might just prove to be the one to break the 'willing horse's' back!

I poured myself another cup of tea and put plenty of sugar in it! I took it through to the lounge and turned on the radio. Perhaps in the cold light of that new day, everything would become clearer and more easily defined. Sitting there in the lounge, drinking my second mug of tea of the morning and listening to the music on the radio, I was contemplating the future and my role as permanent carer for Andy Gange, who had used me so cruelly, vilely and mercilessly. He had caused me such acute agony and major distress over past weeks and months. As Ray Moore's radio show accompanied my thoughts, I considered the whole situation.

It was not as though Andy had no kin to support and help him. In truth, there was his mom, and he had eight sisters and four, or was it five, brothers. They had all turned against him, even his sisters, because of what he had done to me, and none of them felt inclined to want to help him any more. No! Although I had been prepared to forgive - but never forget, oh no, I would never forget - it would seem that his family, especially his lovely mom, who adored me, would never allow him back into their thoughts, let alone the family circle. Surely, in the circumstances, one or other of them ought to take the responsibility for caring for him - not me! Furthermore, if my own family knew anything of what had recently occurred I would not be allowed to take responsibility for his care! I would be pilloried by all of them for even considering such a commitment, particularly in the light of the fact that I had a full-time job, and a very demanding one at that, as well as the fact that I had special needs of my own.

As I finished my tea and went to the kitchen to wash my mug, then returned upstairs to finish getting ready for work, I resolved to talk to members of Andy Gange's family at the earliest possible opportunity, for it ought to be a decision that I took in conjunction with members of that vast clan as to who endeavoured to care for him on his return to the outside world! Why I had never considered that before, I did not know, but at least I had been right. The new day had brought things into a clearer perspective and I now had my thoughts in a much more organised pattern, and could think much more clearly and precisely of the future - a future in which Andy Gange and the permanent care of him might, or might not, come to fruition.

I secured the house, unfurled my white cane and hurried out to catch the bus. As yet, I had heard nothing from Guide Dogs for the Blind, although I had made the application for a guide dog some months previously. I had been told by a woman called Liz McBurney when she telephoned, that someone would be calling to see me in the near future, but that had been in July and, as yet, I had heard nothing further from anyone in regard to this. In the meantime I continued to use 'Old Faithful', and kept hoping each day that I might hear something to my advantage.

I was very much looking forward to having a guide dog.

14

A potted history - 1979 and the eighties.

AFTER THE terrible events that had taken place at the house next door to mine in Rutland Close, Parkside, I never felt happy or comfortable living there again! I had at one time contemplated buying the property if the Labour Government and the borough council ever changed their policies, thus allowing council tenants to engage in home ownership, but following that terrible tragedy, and the aftermath thereof, I did not feel inclined to do so, even though the time was right for such action.

The house at number 25 Rutland Close had been a curiosity for a while, and attracted a lot of visitors. Eventually a gang of louts smashed several windows there, and that caused me to become even more unsettled, despite the lads from the Morleston Estate and the Gunners Lane Academy and Sixth Form College swearing undying devotion and loyalty to me in droves and endless battalions, vowing and declaring how they would 'walk on hot coals in their bare or stockinged feet' for me, and turning up in vast numbers each night to protect me and my home from all would-be assailants, no matter whom or how numerous they were! Needless to say, during their vigils, nobody deigned to attempt to launch an attack upon me or upon the property, but nevertheless, I still felt uncomfortable whenever I was at home those days and wished very much to move. Accordingly, I decided I would do so at the first opportunity.

When Sandy Christmas lost her youngest child, her daughter, Belle, whom she swore was mine, although there was no actual proof, I went up north to Harts Hill to visit her almost immediately. I realised there was no point in pretending. I could not and would not settle down with Sandy and her family, and as I left to return to Gaynsford I made that perfectly clear, even telling her, and I felt lousy doing it, that I had someone else in my life, which was not entirely untrue!

I had met Maura O'Reilly, to whom I was very much attracted, and I was also still seeing, on and off anyway, but seeing her nonetheless, Honey Laverne. Neither of them were my lovers at the time, still, that served to divert the attention of Sandy Christmas from me all together, and I was pleased to have at least one less hassle in my life. I thought perhaps I might buy myself a property and endeavour to do it up with the help of my many friends and acquaintances. I did not have a lot of money to spend, but I could manage to purchase a house if it was reasonably modestly priced and if I thought it would be worthwhile. Accordingly, I began looking around the area.

I found a rather rundown, four-bedroom semi-detached property in Potter Street, off Hyland Road, and went to look at it with a veritable army of my mates! The asking price was £20,000, but the vendors were prepared to drop the price considerably for a quick sale. In the event, I acquired the property for a song, after much haggling and the eventual promise of a cash sale, no solicitors involved and no questions asked. I managed to get the price down to £16,995, and subsequently moved in after a good deal of work had been carried out by armies of my mates, who virtually tore the guts out of it, laying new floors, rewiring, plastering where necessary, decorating all through, laying new carpets, fitting a new bathroom suite and completely fitting out the kitchen with cupboards, a new single sink unit, a brand new cooker etc., etc., in order to make the place more pleasant and habitable. My friend, Barry Smith, who was a chartered surveyor, undertook the survey for me, and he was the one who eventually recommended the price that I paid for the property in Potter Street. Once more, the 'network' wrapped itself around me, and I was afforded a great deal of help and support during my move and the period leading up to that event.

I moved into 55 Potter Street off Hyland Road in Allerton in the late October of 1979. I was sorry to leave Parkside, but at least I was that bit nearer the Family Support Centre on Bread Street, where I was still working as audio typist, switchboard operator and part-time receptionist!

~ ⁊⊷⊰ ~

By the spring of 1980, I had begun to realise how desperately lonely I felt. I contemplated all kinds of things to make my life less lonely. I joined a writers' group that met twice a week, on Monday and Thursday evenings between 6 p.m. and 9 p.m. As a result of my tutoring by members of that group, I produced and indeed had published two books of short stories, one for adults one for children, under the name of Eric Bartholomew. I was quite proud of my efforts in that direction. I also commenced a course in counselling, which involved me in spending one weekend a month for a period of six months in all up in Friskerton, a town some 50 miles north-west of Gaynsford. That was during the spring and summer, into the autumn of 1981.

When I went up there to stay at weekends, usually on a Friday evening, I would stay at the home of Mrs Dorris Wormold. Dorris Wormold was in her sixtieth year when I first met her. A lovely, lively chubby lady with a loud voice, a hearty laugh and a keen sense of humour, she was a widow and the mother of eight children. She had one son still at home, David, who at the time I knew the family was 22 years of age. David was autistic, and not the easiest lad in the world to get along with, but he and I became friends almost from day one, and apparently he fretted when I was not around. Dorris had one other son, Alan, and six daughters, Shirley, Hazel, Jean, Valerie, Pamela and Caroline. All six girls were married, but Valerie was in process of a divorce. She worked in a factory as a machine operator and had four sons. She was 32 years old when I first met her.

Valerie had a heart as big as a whale, and her body was of similar proportions! Valerie Leask weighed in excess of 19 stone and stood about five feet tall in her stockinged feet. She decided that she had a lover's crush on yours truly. All Dorris's family were very friendly towards me and treated me well whenever I went up to stay with them, but Valerie Leask definitely had designs upon me, and saw me as 'husband number two' and father to her four erring offspring, Peter, James, Richard and William! I really was not interested, not in the least. Granted, she was a wonderful cook. She made me cakes and bread pudding, and entertained me to dinner and tea at her house, which, although poor and rather shabby, was nevertheless clean and as tidy as a house with four young lads in it could possibly be.

Valerie worked five days per week and sometimes on a Saturday morning until around lunchtime, so she did not get a lot of time to herself. As I say, she was a very friendly young woman, but she came on too strong for me, and eventually I was forced to beat a somewhat hasty retreat from the town of Friskerton before the sound of wedding bells assailed my ears and I found myself being dragged forcibly down the aisle by that larger than life human being!

By that time I had completed the course on which I had embarked, and had received my qualification as a Counsellor, Stage One, and had gained my certificate to prove it, which I had framed and proudly took back to the Family Support Centre to display in my office. It was up on the wall above my desk. The following year I obtained my Stage Two Counselling Certificate and in 1983, my Stage Three. Naturally, as my skills improved I was given more work and higher status within the Family Support Centre, but although I had tribes of friends, and kept in touch with my own family and indeed my late wife's family, Liz, her mother was now deceased, but her Aunt Annie had married, I still felt desperately lonely.

I eventually decided to take in students from the Sixth Form College on Gunners Lane. At one time I had as many as a dozen young men sharing my accommodation with me. I slept downstairs on a double put-you-up sofa in the main sitting room. I had two other put-you-up sofas in the living room on which two young blokes slept. The four bedrooms were given over to the other ten lads, who shared them - I had two sets of bunk beds in each of the two larger ones, and a single bed in the other two smaller rooms, and that was how we managed.

Unfortunately I was still not happy! The situation worked against me. The place was always crowded out with young people and, although I did not mind that initially, eventually the sheer numbers of young men in the house at any one time began to pall. They would often arrive home drunk, bringing hordes of their equally drunken mates along with them. The fighting and arguing would then commence, and the police frequently had to be called to sort out the rioting that went on at my house in Potter Street, which in itself was extremely embarrassing!

Other characteristics of their communal behaviour irked me and caused me considerable distress. They would leave the sink full of dirty pots, they would throw their clothes all over the house, and shoes were merely discarded anywhere and everywhere. They would never clean the bath or shower after using them, and often they did not flush the toilet after use. Several of their number smoked, and I regularly came home to find the place swarming with young men, often half-naked, ashtrays full to overflowing and the whole atmosphere within the house full of choking smoke!

I would prepare meals because they would say they would be in, but nobody would come home until late, and when they did so, they did not want whatever food I had cooked for their consumption. I even had goods stolen from me, in quantity, which finally tipped the balance for me. The final straw that broke the back of this 'willing horse' came after one long, delightful Sunday that I had spent in the park at the other end of town.

In the mid to late evening I returned home to find the house absolutely heaving with students, even more queueing to get inside, music blaring out so loud you could hear it before you reached the end of the street, and a gang of neighbours assembled, threatening all kinds of dour consequences if I did not do something immediately to rectify the situation! I was absolutely furious! I descended upon the throng of students like the Demon King! They were smoking pot - cannabis - injecting drugs, drinking out of bottles, including several bottles of my best Scotch whisky, the music was blaring out for all to hear, there were fights going on all over the place and there was even sexual activity going on in almost every room, including my bedroom, where at least a dozen young males were cavorting on my king-size bed!

I was beside myself with rage, and this culminated in my shouting fit to beat the band! I ordered every single individual out of the house, throwing their clothes and other belongings out after them until there was nothing left to throw! I then called the police, who came around and ensured that I was left in peace.

A couple of days later two of my windows were smashed in retaliation for what I had done, and later on my door was daubed with dog faeces! I was utterly horrified! I decided there and then that I would sell the property for whatever I could get, and in the event, I made a profit of over £10,000 on the sale price I had paid.

§·••·§

I had attained all my counselling qualifications up to Stage Three and had decided that, as I was selling the property at 55 Potter Street, I might as well make a clean break of it and leave Gaynsford. Accordingly, I applied for, and was lucky enough to obtain, a job as a counseller in Stanborough, which was just 20 miles south-east of Harts Hill, where my sister, Doreen, and all her family resided. That was in the late autumn of 1984.

The Prospect Estate in Stanborough was a poor, rundown overpopulated area, very similar to Allerton, and I soon found myself feeling right at home there! The people were poor, shabby and mostly out of work, but they had hearts of gold and, like those in Allerton, if they liked you then you were 'in'. If they did not care for you then the best thing to do was get out o' town fast! I almost immediately settled into life in that rundown, dilapidated chaotic area of the new town in which I found myself, and greatly enjoyed the work on the vast Prospect Estate, which was multiple and varied. I arrived in Stanborough during the Autumn of 1984, and left just over two years later.

My move took me further north to the City of Sunderford. In Sunderford, that great, sprawling bustling city of the northeast, I worked mainly on the Thrush Hall Estate and also on the Gannimede Estate, as well as in the Tinsel Bank area. I also worked for long periods at the Arndale Youth Custody Centre, just north-east of Sunderford. That institution at the time housed around 450 youths and young men who were waiting to move into youth wings in adult prisons. I spent a great deal of my time working among those young men, many of whom were homeless, rootless and had innumerable problems cluttering up their lives. The work was essentially very rewarding.

I loved Sunderford, a great city, and later on I moved back there to live permanently, but that is another tale, and will keep for another time. I was happy working in that vibrant city, and I did so until the spring of 1988. In the April of that year, at the commencement of the new school term, I moved once again. That time I took a job in the south-east of the country, down in Langham in Essex. I was offered a position as counsellor in residence at the Whiteleys School for Boys in Taplin Park, Langham, Essex. It was a vast establishment wherein at least 650 boys boarded, and another 500 or so attended as day pupils. Later, the premises were extended to take in around 1,000 boarders, and the day facility was greatly reduced to around 350, mostly older lads who went in daily for training in the workshops etc.

When I arrived, I spent some time with the headmaster, Mr Tucker, and his deputy, Mr Cochran, learning about the job I was expected to undertake, the scale of the work, the numbers of pupils within the establishment and the fact that, basically, I would be heading up a team of counsellors, but they were all part-timers who went in during the week, and I was the only resident counsellor. I would need to be on call 24-7 because there were a great many lads who would need my help! Of course, I would get school holidays and one weekend off per term, at around the half-term stage. The money was not wonderful; but I felt I could cope with that, and the challenge the work would provide certainly appealed.

The boys and young men at that establishment, aged from eight to 19 years, were either disabled in some way, mostly physical or visual, or else they were audibly impaired, but there were also a number of slow learners among their number, and many of the lads were maladjusted, with quite severe behavioural and emotional problems. Thus, my job was going to be exciting, varied and constant, and, as I soon discovered, practically never-ending! Boys and young men simply queued outside my room from dawn to dusk and beyond, or so it seemed to me, with hardly any respite, and they all needed a 'crutch'; someone to lean upon, someone to offer them constant support, even affection, and protection not only from one another, but from themselves!

There at Whiteleys, my life was constantly plagued by boys, youths and young men, and whenever I took a break it was more than welcome! Even at weekends, when I went out walking in order to try and get some time alone, or just to have some thinking time to myself, I was often pursued by seemingly endless numbers of youngsters.

"Where you goin, Sir?" they would chorus, and then they would commence following in limitless numbers, calling out to their vast tribes of mates.

"Cum on, Boyzie's goin' aht! Let's go wi' 'im, guys!"

I would end up walking along the road like the Pied Piper, with vast armies of lads struggling to follow in my wake! In truth, it all eventually became too much, for I hardly ever had a moment to myself, and in the end it had a profound effect upon my life, and led to my early exit from the school on health grounds. I worked at Whiteleys School from mid-April of 1988 and the beginning of the long summer term until the early part of February 1989.

The events that finally culminated in my leaving the establishment occurred about four weeks into the spring term. I collapsed while at work one morning, suffering from burnout and complete and utter exhaustion. It all happened on a Wednesday morning in early February, following a long and arduous staff meeting. I was in a room simply packed out, stacked out with lads, with a queue outside a mile and a half long and growing! I was in process of counselling a particularly difficult young man, a very strong and aggressive epileptic, Kevin Duffy. Suddenly, the whole room seemed to commence spinning around. I could feel myself falling! Kevin Duffy, a big lad and, as I say, usually very difficult and often aggressive, quickly realised I was in trouble. He moved behind me to catch me as I fell. Suddenly I was falling backwards then I was on the floor, sprawling at his feet.

Kevin, who possessed great strength, but very little in the way of commonsense, lifted me up from the dirty floor and held me safely in his strong arms, leaning me backwards so that my head was planted against his chest. Other older boys flocked behind me to help and support him while even more excitable, almost hysterical youngsters gathered around, crowding in on all sides in such a vastness of numbers, squeezing and squashing in tighter, tighter, much tighter all around us! The noise was deafening as everyone tried to get close enough to help, or to find out what was wrong with me. Apparently the staff had all on to get into the room to assist me because of the vast numbers of youngsters who were crammed, jammed in there, with their inherent desire to protect me and look after me!

In truth, the lads at Whiteleys, almost to a man, revered and worshipped me, which was brought home to me when it became clear that I would have to relinquish my duties at the school! Two teachers and a vast crowd of the older lads eventually helped me into the staffroom, and the doctor was summoned. As a consequence of what had occurred, I was taken by ambulance into hospital in Langham.

I managed to phone my brother, Eric, from the hospital. He could not come down, but said he would let Mum and Dad know what had happened and where I was to be found. He expressed his sympathy and said if I was not out of the hospital by the weekend, he and Eve would come down to visit me. However, he reckoned as how Mum and Dad would want me home with them, and as it transpired, he was right.

That was on the Wednesday, and a week the following Saturday, in the afternoon, my parents arrived to take me back home to their place in Gaynsford, back home to good old California Road. I remained with Mum and Dad for three weeks, after which time I went up to Harts Hill to stay with Doreen and Fred Dingle. While I was staying there, I saw quite a bit of Sandy Christmas's cousin, Norma Townley, and her family.

I wrote to the council in Gaynsford, North Midlands, saying that I was returning to live there, and wondering if perhaps I might be lucky enough to obtain the tenancy of a council flat, or even a one-bedroom bungalow somewhere. I also wrote a long beseeching letter to Councillor Marjorie McNault. Despite the fact that she was now well into her seventieth year, Councillor McNault, still spritely, was busier than ever undertaking her work as a councillor in the Allerton area. She was still a great friend of mine, and we often corresponded. I had high hopes that she might be able to 'pull a few strings' legitimately, of course, as she was about to become mayor of the town, to help me in my quest to return to Gaynsford.

෨෨෨

Once more my wishes came to fruition. I received a letter from the director of housing in Gaynsford, one Mr Simon Parker. Mr Parker said he remembered me, that there was a house in the Osleston area of the town, a two-bedroom council dwelling on

Milling Street, of which I could have the tenancy if I wished. There were some repairs required to be undertaken to the property, but if I notified him within a very short space of time, those could be implemented and he would set the wheels in motion. That was on a Wednesday in May of 1989.

On the following Saturday, I received notification from the housing department in Gaynsford that if I arrived there at 9 a.m. that coming Monday morning and asked to see Mike Banner or Eileen Weir, I would be given the keys to the property in Milling Street, plus the rent book and all other relevant documents to enable me to take on the tenancy of the house! I was informed that all necessary repairs had been undertaken, and that I could move in as soon as I desired to do so! Goal! Of course, there was some decoration internally that would need attending to, plus I would need a phone installing. I would require other small alterations to be undertaken, but those could be done in the fullness of time and would be easily achieved with the assistance of my mates in the 'network' that still wrapped itself around me in that sprawling town of the North Midlands!

I was going home! I was over the moon and decided to travel back to Gaynsford on the Sunday. Accordingly, I caught a train back to my old home, and temporarily stayed at the home of my late wife's nephew, David. I had kept in touch with Susan's family over the years, and my nephew and I had always been the very best of pals. Davey was more than happy to put me up for a few days, at least until the house in Milling Street was sorted out.

On arrival back in Gaynsford, I found there were no end of people still there who remembered me and were only too ready to help me become reinstalled within the town and within the new locality and the community in which I would soon reside. There I was, once again back 'home' in Gaynsford, North Midlands.

৻৶৶

In the mid-June of 1989, I visited the studios of Sunny Gold Radio, the sunniest sound around, and was offered the post of presenter, with a fortnight's training course in order to qualify. I had had experience of working for hospital radio in the past over a period of several years. My tastes in music were wide and varied, and I had always thoroughly enjoyed being involved in the presentation of programmes on the hospital networks. They could tell immediately that I had a flair for broadcasting, and instantly offered me the 'Night Shift', Monday through to Saturday, from midnight to 6 a.m. Once my training was complete later, I also acquired an afternoon show, 'Afternoon Delight' on a Sunday, so I was kept pretty busy.

At the culmination of the decade, I had undertaken the 80-hour music marathon, at the end of which my erstwhile lover, now turned cruel adversary, had finally caught up with me and had stabbed me and beaten me over the head, fully intending to kill me! If it hadn't been for the wonderful help from friends and acquaintances, the police, Father Martyn, who had been a marvellous friend indeed, plus all the good wishes, cards, phone calls, visits etc., from my family, from fans who had enjoyed the 80-hour music marathon, and the incredible help and support I received from the staff at the County Hospital, I should not have been alive to write down any of these events! Luckily, Johnnie's plans did not come to fruition. Instead, after stabbing me so heartlessly and cruelly, and hitting me over the head with the heavy object she used, she was tackled and brought to the ground by members of the police force and also the security guards who were based at the premises of Sunny Gold Radio.

I had hoped one day to have my day in court with Johnnie Friscoe, and although I survived her violent and virulent attacks upon me, the case never came to court! She had been examined by four eminent psychiatrists after being taken to Fair Lawn Psychiatric Unit at Broadlands Hospital in Shenley in the home counties, and they all pronounced her 'unfit to plead'. She was then moved into the secure unit at Craig Moor Hospital in Cruttherland, North-West Scotland. In 1992, Johnquel Amelia Friscoe was found hanged in her room in that wild and remote place! She had made three different attempts on my life, all for love, or so she said, and at one time I had believed myself to be head over heels in love with her, but I did not shed any tears when I knew she was dead. No! I could not feel sad for her, not like I had done for my darling Susan, or for Paul McGowan, or for my dear friend Rob McCallasky, or even for poor Bessie Starling, who had been so cruelly murdered by her drunken beast of a husband in the house next door to me in Rutland Close. No! I shed no tears for Johnnie Friscoe, but I kept the memories of our lovemaking safe within my heart, and I often thought back to the happy days and the good times we had spent together, especially that wonderful day in August 1978 when we went racing around the track at Brawnstone in Northants. A wonderful, happy time for both of us

Poor Johnnie sits a-weeping, a-weeping, a-weeping,
Poor Johnnie sits a-weeping on a bright summer day.

Why do you sit a-weeping, a-weeping, a-weeping,
Why do you sit a-weeping on this bright summer day?

I'm weeping for a playmate...

❧

What of the family during the eighties and the early to mid-nineties, the Thatcher and the Major years? Well, first of all, let me speak of my late wife's family in Gaynsford.

In 1982, Sue's mother, Liz, died very suddenly after a short illness brought on by a fall while she was out in town. She had apparently been dismounting from a bus when the vehicle started to move, and she fell her length in the middle of the road. The bus dragged her for several hundred yards before stopping, and Liz was rushed to the College Hospital because it was the nearest and they were on call that day. She was subsequently transferred to the County Hospital, and I received a phone call from Dave, my late wife's nephew, to let me know she was domiciled there and asking for me.

I visited, but Liz was too far gone to know me. They put her on a life support system and five days later they turned it off. Her injuries were quite horrific I was told, and I was extremely upset by her demise. Liz had been a good and a pleasant mother-in-law, always ready to help if called upon to do so. She had mourned the loss of her daughter, Sue, and also the tragic loss, soon after our marriage, of her husband, Frank, who had died in 1971. He was 12 years older than his wife and had died of a heart attack while at work in the foundry where he had been employed for many years.

"He hardly ever had a day off sick," moaned Liz at his funeral. "He didn't even like having time off for holidays he loved his work so much!"

Frank Smith had been far from being a saint! When he had first learned that his daughter, Sue, wished to marry me, he had blazed:

"Yo' canna marry 'im, lass! Aw wan' yo' te 'av someone to look arter yo', aw dunna wan' yo' lookin' arter a jockin' cripple all your jockin' life! Aw won't 'av it! Yo' ain't gonna marry 'im, an' that's that!"

He had expected Sue to cower down and submit to his harsh and unremitting demands, but surprisingly, and to his great annoyance and total amazement, she had adamantly and staunchly refused to bow down.

"I've already accepted him, so you had better get used to it, Daddy dear!" she said with a scathing look that could wither the leaves on the trees. "Now, I'm going upstairs!"

Apparently, he had chased her up the stairs and she had locked herself in her room, terrified of the recriminations that might follow her revelations about her impending marriage, however, after a while Frank had calmed down, and when I went up to Gaynsford to visit the family for the first time, in the early Autumn of 1965, he was very friendly towards me, almost conspiratorial at times.

On the Saturday afternoon, while Sue and her mom went over

to see Alice and Joe Cunliffe, Frank and I sat together in the backyard, overlooked by the apple tree and the dying plum tree, which he had cosseted all its life, and drank beer from half-pint tankards.

"Where will yo' live, son?" he had asked me.

I had my answer ready immediately without having to think at all.

"Oh, I shall move up here, of course!" I told him. "I have no wish to live down in the Smoke."

That had seemed to partially appease Frank, who got up, took my half-pint mug, went back into the kitchen, refilled both mugs and returned to his seat in the yard, pushing my mug across the garden table at which we were both seated.

"Cheers! Gud 'ealth to yo', son, an' aw 'ope as 'ow ye'll both be very 'appy in your marriage! Dawn't forget, if there's owt yo' need, yo' on'y 'av te ask, an' if aw con 'elp yo' in ony way, then aw will an' all!"

I smiled to myself when he said that. In the event, the only time I ever asked Frank for help, he refused me and, therefore, I never repeated the exercise! I was sorry when he died in the spring of 1971 at the age of 66 years. Frank had had a heart attack whilst engaged in his work in the foundry, and he had been rushed to the County Hospital. Unfortunately, they could do nothing to save him, and he was pronounced dead on arrival at the accident and emergency department. Lizzie was sent for, and she and Aunt Annie went over too, from where they telephoned Sue, who subsequently called me. We went over, but as there was nothing anyone could do, we did not remain there for long.

The funeral was a sad little affair - loads of his mates from work, and the immediate family, plus the extended family on Lizzie's side, as far as we knew them at that time. Frank had a sister, Vera, and a brother, Norman, but neither of them went to his funeral. Apparently Lizzie had fallen out with them, and there had been no communication between them for years, so that was that, and all about it. Frank had loved his job so much that he had worked two years over his allotted time, and had been allowed to do so, after all, he was one of the best woodcutters they had ever had, according to Joe Forkin, his foreman, who frequently visited Lizzie after Frank's death and had hoped to get it together with her initially, but it was not to be!

Lizzie virtually died when her husband did in 1971, and although she lasted another 11 years, she never really came alive again after his decease. She too was now dead! Only Trudy, Mick and their son, Dave, were left of the nuclear family into which I had married, but what of the extended family?

Well, Lizzie's elder sister, Annie, had met and subsequently married Albert John Higgins. They had first met at a club for people who wished to learn old-time dancing! They had danced together from 2 p.m. until around 4 p.m. with a break for tea and biscuits at around 2.50 p.m. Annie had thoroughly enjoyed both the exercise and the warm friendly conversation in which she had engaged with her dancing partner, Albert, who insisted that she call him Bertie! Bertie Higgins, who was three years younger than Annie, had lost his wife, Maisie, to cancer about 18 months before. He had just started picking up the pieces of his life again, and was now looking forward to a rosier future, getting out and about more.

Bertie had bought himself a motorcycle, a 650cc Civic, and he invited Aunt Annie to ride home on the back of it. She was somewhat unsure at first, but later, when she was cajoled gently into submission, she did not exactly fight back! In a whirlwind of laughter and with slight misgivings, Annie was driven home on the back of Bertie's motorcycle, and she laughed all the way home, according to her new paramour.

Less than six months later, in the autumn of 1980, the couple became engaged. There was a big party to celebrate at the Old-Time Dancing Club where they had first met. Everyone in the family attended except for Lizzie, Annie's sister. Lizzie was mortified that Annie should consent to marry such a person as Albert (Bertie) Higgins, whom Lizzie considered to be far too low-class ever to enter into such an arrangement with her sister! Annie, who possessed a wicked sense of humour, thought it was a huge joke that her sister should think it so low-class of her to be marrying a bloke like Bertie Higgins, who had been a chimney sweep in the past, and now undertook a window cleaning round to keep his hand in, even though he was well into his sixties. Lizzie made her feelings very clear by not attending either the engagement party for Aunt Annie, or her subsequent wedding at the register office in the town square, opposite the county court.

The wedding took place in the early spring of 1981, and the couple honeymooned for two glorious weeks in Macclesborough, North Yorkshire. Trudy, Mick, Dave and I all attended Annie's wedding, along with numerous friends, and we all had a great time celebrating the marriage between Annie Cunliffe and Albert John Higgins, the chimney sweep, known to all as Bertie. Only Lizzie stayed in the background. She remained at home, fuming at the stupidity of her sister allowing herself to be dragooned into a relationship with 'someone like that'. The rift between the two sisters, who had previously always been so close, was never really healed because Lizzie Smith, mother of my lovely late wife, Sue, died the following year.

Trudy and Mick continued to live where they had always lived, in their crowded off-street terraced house with all their dogs, birds, fish, ferrets etc., and Mick also kept racing pigeons in the backyard. He was a happy-go-lucky, come day, go day, kind of bloke, and as long as his wife was there to see to his daily requirements, to cook, wash, clean etc. for him and to ensure that he was happy and comfortable, and as long as he was there to do all the gardening, decorating, repairs to the house etc., etc., and make sure the cars were running okay, as long as he gave Trudy his wage packet each week, and as long as she undertook all the shopping and paid all the bills, those two people, who thought the world of one another, rubbed along very happily and contentedly, thank you very much!

What of their son, Davey? Well, in 1983 he met and subsequently married a lovely girl called Nancie. Nan, as everyone called her, was three years older than Davey. She was an absolute sweetheart, and the couple had three smashing children, James, Richard and Helen. Davey deserved to be happy, and he was.

At Liz's funeral, we discovered other family members whom nobody had seen or heard of for years. Ada, Lizzie and Annie's aunt, the sister of their mother, who was 90 plus, attended with her two daughters, Olive and Ivy, plus their husbands, Jim and Gerry. They had travelled down from Blackwell in Lancashire, and were determined to stay around for a while and 'get to knaw' us all. Ada turned out to be quite a character. She could play the penny whistle and also read teacups, which she did for all of us before she and her family left to head back up north.

The reason no one had heard of them for years was because there had been a big row between Alice Cunliffe and her sister, Ada, and that had culminated in Ada storming out of the house and declaring she would never set foot in it again while her sister, Alice, lived. Harsh words, but she had stuck to her word! She had now made contact once more with the rest of the family, and wished very much to be present at the funeral of her late niece, Lizzie. In truth, it was good to meet that wonderful old lady who was 95 years young, and such a totally different person from her sister, Alice, whose sole joy appeared to be being miserable! I know that sounds like a contradiction in terms, but nevertheless, as far as that woman was concerned, it was the truth.

Alice and Joe Cunliffe were probably the most miserable old couple I have ever had the misfortune to know, and I have met some miserable old people in my time, believe me! I got along well enough with the newly found relations, and in fact, Trudy, Mick and I went up to Blackwell to see them before Aunt Ada died in 1986, just two years short of her century - a wonderful old lady! It was a pleasure and a privilege to have known her, even for a short period of time.

We remained in contact with the two cousins and their families, and it was good to have involvement with an extended family, even if the various factions did not see much of one another. How stupid families are, keeping up grudges for years, but then, most families seem to have some kind of major problem within their family circle, which always leads to confrontation and often to long-term feuding! My own family, on my father's side, is no exception, but to conclude the saga of my late wife's nuclear and extended family.

Trudy and Mick remained in the house into which they had moved just after their marriage. Mick was very keen on gardening, decorating etc., and they kept the place in pristine condition, albeit it was often untidy, but never ever dirty! Mick had married well. Even his late father, Frank, had approved of Trudy, and why would he not? She was attractive, vivacious, personable and homely, and she was a brilliant cook, a kind and considerate daughter-in-law and a superb hostess. In truth, Trudy Blackstock was a splendid catch and was admired by many lads in and around the area. Michael Smith was considered a lucky bloke to have won her hand in matrimony, and he knew it too! His mates all envied him and went to the house in vast numbers to meet his new wife. They literally swarmed to his house - in truth, Mick said he had never realised he had so many mates! Trudy, who was certainly a looker in her day and could have had her pick of anyone she cared to choose, only had eyes for one man - *her* man, Michael Francis Smith!

David, their only son, had married well, and they adored Nan and the three children. Davey purchased a house in Osleston - number 5 Carole Crescent on the Brontae Estate - and he and his father did it up so that it was fit for a queen, which was how young Davey thought of his wife, Nancie. They were very happy, and I saw a good deal of them once I returned to live in Gaynsford after my years away.

What of my own vast clan? Well, at the end of the eighties, my parents, Mary and George, caused shock waves through the family circle when they suddenly announced at a wedding gathering for one of Nelly and Alf's children, or some such event, they were buying a bungalow and moving to Portman on the Isle of Wight. They subsequently did so and never looked back.

My Uncle Len, Aunt Joyce's husband, died of a heart attack in 1985, and Joyce was desolate! By that time both their sons, Gary and Terry, had married their girlfriends, Karen (Kaz) and Patricia (Trish), and had set up homes in Clayborough, Kent, and Totleigh in Gloucestershire respectively. Both had families. Joyce spent time with both her sons and their families while she made up her mind what she would do now that she was widowed. The last thing she wished to do was to be a burden to either of them, and in the end she made her decision. Following my Aunt Betty and Uncle Bill's move to Klee Sands in North Lincolnshire, where they bought a boarding house, Aunt Joyce decided to contact the council in Scampton, just across the river from Klee Sands, to see if she could arrange for an exchange with someone in that area who might want to move to London. Aunt Joyce moved north to Scampton and spent her time, a greater part of it anyway, helping her sister, Betty, and my cousin, Anne, to run the boarding house in Klee Sands, a popular seaside resort in North Lincolnshire.

Nelly and Alf Sunley remained in Seaport until the end of the eighties, when they moved to a three-bedroom bungalow in Slade. Queenie, with her husband, Matt, and their four children, took over the running of the Seaways Guest House in Seaport. Cathy, the next eldest daughter, who had married a fellow called Ben, helped Queenie to run that establishment and apparently they made quite a success of it in time.

My Uncle Sid and his mate, Ernie, continued to run their taxi service in Seaport and the surrounding area, and they had quite a considerable fleet of vehicles in the end. Sid loved all of it, and he also loved his motorbikes, of which he owned five. Sid's wife, Brenda, was a good cook and housekeeper, and his best friend in all the world, and they both lived very busy and active lives. He ran the business and enjoyed making the acquaintance of new customers, often in pubs and clubs in the area, whilst she was a grand hostess whenever he held parties at the house they had purchased in Gypsy Lane on the fringes of Slade. She also involved herself in the life of the local women's institute, where she made many friends. She was a writer, mostly of poetry and short stories for children, and she worked four mornings per week in a nursery where she helped with packing plants, watering produce, preparing orders of flowers for local florists and also for export to countries all over the five continents. She loved the work. She also enjoyed painting, mostly watercolour, and maintained a great interest in flowers and gardening, and she and Sid had two allotments where they grew all their own vegetables etc., and also kept chickens and a goat! They were blissfully happy, and I was glad for Sid, who was a lovely guy and deserved all the happiness that he eventually gained from his life with Brenda.

My brother, Eric, and his wife, Eve, moved from their beautiful house in Cherry Wootton in 1986, and went to live in Leaming Cross in South Lincolnshire. Eric was still very busy and Yvonne seemed to live as full a life as he did. There was always something going on for them, or so it seemed anyway. Their son, Micky, married a girl called Alison, and they had one daughter, Abbigail. My parents thought the world of her, as indeed did Eve and Eric. He fairly doted on his granddaughter, and was fiercely protective of her. Five years after their marriage, Micky and Ali split up and eventually divorced. Micky met and married a girl called Lynette, and they had two children, Thomas and Rosie. They lived in Shirston, about 20 miles from Leaming Cross. Abbigail went and stayed with Micky and his new family for part of every summer holiday and Christmas every other year, and they also saw her once a month for a weekend. It all seemed fairly amicable, but it caused Eve and Eric a good deal of sorrow and soul-searching, especially whenever they had to say goodbye to their eldest granddaughter, whom they idolised.

Micky and his new family were very happy, and Lynette was a grand girl of Irish extraction, full of the blarney and very well thought of by all the family. Micky, Eve and Eric's son, had married his first wife in the spring of 1991, and he married Lynette in the autumn of 1997, following his divorce. Rosie, their second child, was born in the Year 2000, and with regard to my sister, Doreen, and her clan - well!

In 1978, following the birth of their thirteenth child, a daughter, Muriel, named after our Aunt Muriel, Dad's only sister, our Dorrie swore an oath that there would be no more additions to that vast and growing tribe. Despite that, in April of 1983, she gave birth to a ten pound baby boy! Doreen and Fred were thrilled to little mint-balls with their new son, and Doreen immediately announced that he would be called Eric. Her twin brother and his wife went up to Harts Hill for the christening, and so did I. Eric had a fine pair of lungs on him and Doreen and Fred were so proud of their new son! He was the last of their 14 children, and despite weighing in at just over ten pounds and his good strong physique, his loud cries and his seemingly rapid development, Eric was found to have Down's syndrome. He was diagnosed as being low grade, so he was not as handicapped as many who have the condition. Nevertheless, his special need made Eric a rather difficult and truculent child at times, although when he was happy and affectionate, he was a real smasher.

I adored him, and we became big mates almost from day one. He called me 'Ersie', because he could not say my name properly, and he loved to sit on my knee whenever I visited. He enjoyed playing with cars and loved riding in them, and also on the tractors and his Dad's motorbikes. Eric was a clown. He loved making people laugh, and he was a bit of a daredevil. When he became older, he raised a lot of money for charities involved with 'special needs' children by undertaking all kinds of mad pursuits, and he loved to do that. He left school at 14, and helped his dad with the pigs, which he thoroughly enjoyed, but now I am jumping ahead of myself again! One step at a time, Boyzie! One step at a time, mate!

With regard to the rest of Doreen and Fred's large family, by 1990, Peggy Sue, Frank, June, Arthur and Ellen were all married and had families. Peggy Sue had married at 16 years, and by the end of 1990 she had eight children! Frank had five, June and Arthur each had three. Ellen, or Nell as she was known, had two sets of twins in less than a year! Doreen and Fred's twin boys, Jackie and Freddie, lived at home and worked alongside Fred on the farm, loving every minute of it. They grew into strong, fit healthy teenagers, both six-footers, and they remained single until they were well into their late twenties. Iris, Gordon and his 3 younger brothers, grew up fast, and Doreen and Fred were inordinately proud of their large brood.

Muriel, who until the arrival of Eric had been the youngest, proved a bit of a handful once Eric had arrived on the scene, and needed that extra bit special care. Muriel rebelled, and was sent to live with her Grannie June for a while, then later with her Grannie Muriel, her namesake. Both grannies were quite strict with the little girl, and did not allow her to get away with very much. Muriel became quite a difficult child, and in her teens she was extremely wayward. Of all the 14 children of Doreen and Fred, their Muriel was probably the most troublesome. She ran away a couple of times, once to London, once to France, but she was taken off the plane in Paris because she had no passport. On her return to England, she spent a short spell in the care of the North-East District Council. At the time, she was not even 12 years old!

Eventually, Muriel calmed down, but not before she had been 'on the street', had tried soft drugs and had been picked up drunk on several occasions under age! She certainly was a handful, but all that was much later on. Yes! During the eighties and the early nineties, life within the family went on and many events occurred - some good, some not so good - but all of them of note and of particular significance within the circle of my nuclear and extended families.

15

Saturday, 3rd November 1990.

I WAS VERY tired! I had not been to bed until well after 2 a.m.
and it was now just four hours later, but I had to move! I had a
lot to do before 10 a.m. when Bob Douse of Phoenix Cars was
due to arrive. When he did so, I had to go shopping, and then at
around 12.30 p.m. I would arrive to pick up Andy from the convalescent unit at the College Hospital and take him back to Milling
Street.

We had been so busy those last few weeks just preparing for
his arrival there. The council had been wonderful. No, truly! I
have to give praise where praise was due. They had been incredible, and nothing had been too much trouble for their building
department, their electricians, plumbers etc., etc. Everyone has
dovetailed well and gelled together. The standard of work they
had carried out at my house in Milling Street had been of the
highest, and I had made many new friends during the course of
all that work. Hopefully, everything was now ready to welcome
Andy back home, but I was still feeling apprehensive.

We had a downstairs toilet for him and a shower room. We had
made the dining room into a bed-sitting room, and that was completely accessible for Andy's use. We still had the big lounge, and
the kitchen was well equipped. I didn't have a conservatory on the
back, but we had made it so that we could wheel Andy's chair out
of the back door of the kitchen straight down into the large con-

crete yard with trees and a small rockery at the bottom.

There was a greenhouse in that big yard, and five sheds that I had inherited when I moved in. I was quite delighted with the property, which was big. There were three good-sized rooms downstairs, plus the new facilities for Andy's exclusive use. I had the bathroom, shower and toilet upstairs. There were two good-sized bedrooms upstairs as well as the separate bathroom with a shower, which used to be a bedroom apparently, hence its size, and a separate toilet. Yes! All in all, I had done well to acquire that property at 30 Milling Street.

We had had a stairlift installed to enable Andy to get up and down the stairs should he so desire .He would have to climb onto the seat and sit there while he pressed buttons, one of which took him up the stairs, one of which brought the apparatus down again! It was quite revolutionary. I had seen one at the convalescent unit and asked if it was possible to have one installed in my house. When the council said they would pay for it, I decided to have it, and I was glad I did, although perhaps it did look slightly incongruous, jutting out as it sat at the foot of the stairs. However, if it helped Andy to live a more independent and active life, well then it was worth it in my opinion.

Andy's family were coming around to his residing at Milling Street with me, but it took some time for them all to become used to the idea, and nobody was very enthusiastic about it. Still, they would all help, they had told me, and would ensure that things ran as smoothly as possible once the move took place and Andy was settled in my new home.

I hoped the time spent at 30 Milling Street would be a happy time for me. I loved my job, and it was going real well. I had made some good friends, especially Otis Masher, also Liz Lane, but Wes Pritchard had left us. He went after six months, and had returned to Wales to work and live because his family was homesick. Jeremiah Johnson had also moved on, but more of that anon.

I had to get up and dressed, wash, shave, cook myself some breakfast, then prepare for my shopping expedition and then it would be time to collect Andy and bring him home! I heaved myself out of bed and began to prepare for the day to come. I showered and shaved in the large and rather chilly bathroom. I decided that I would buy new bathmats, a bathroom set, some new toothbrushes, toothpaste, toothbrush holders, a new soap dish, a toilet roll holder that I could screw in etc. I had a good deal of shopping to do that day! After my shave, my shower and my other ablutions, I went back into the bedroom to dress.

I turned the radio on. I like to have music to listen to when I first rise in the morning, it sets me up for the day, at least that's what I find anyway. I know some people can't stand to have music on while they get ready for work or whatever, but I must have music wherever I am in the house. It soothes me when I feel savage and it bucks me up when I feel dejected and miserable. That day I just felt great apprehension. Yes, I know! I had decided to have Andy back there to live with me. I need not have done so. Many people said I was a fool to even contemplate having him to stay with me, but I felt I owed it to him. I felt I owed him the chance to have some sort of life - some form of independence - and with me I hoped that was what he would get and also that it was what he would want! I knew there would undoubtedly be problems. Andy still had difficulties when walking. He became tired very quickly, which could lead to ultimate frustration and also belligerence on his part, and sometimes to downright aggression, even violence! I was ready for him! Yes, I was all geared up and ready for him if he 'came it', as my late Grannie Annie would have put it. I had a feeling she was watching over me that day, which was borne out because of a dream I had had the previous night.

It had been a weird dream, and as I padded downstairs, drew curtains, put the kettle on to make a pot of tea, unlocked and unbolted the doors, fed Minnie, my cat that I had recently acquired, or should I perhaps say she had acquired me, and also undertook other jobs I needed to do, like flicking a duster around, feeding the fish I had also acquired, although for the life of me I did not know why because I could not see them, I thought about the strange dream I had experienced.

§❧§

Dream Sequence.

In my dream it seemed as though I was back once more at the Seaways Guest House in the coastal town of Seaport, down in West Sussex. That had been the home of my late and still lamented Grannie Annie and her family for years, and when the children grew up and left home, she had taken in male lodgers for whom she cooked, cleaned, washed, ironed etc., etc., and she swore that she loved every minute of it! She had about eight lodgers living in the house for many years, including a concert pianist, an artist, a spot-welder, an electrician, a plumber, a guy who owned most of the slot machines in the arcades, a guy who worked on the fairground, and Stan!

Stan Vardy had been with her for years, more or less ever since the time my Grandad Walter passed away. I never remember my Grandad Walter, but my twin brother and sister and I positively adored 'Uncle Stan' Vardy, or 'Grandpa Stan' as we later came to call him! He had died in July of 1960, at the commencement of that long hot summer during which I suddenly found out that my parents were actually human beings after all and not the ultimate super-gods I had believed them to be in the early years of my childhood.

Back to my dream! In the dream I was back at Seaways, and it was some time in the mid to late 1960s. Most of the family on my mother's side, were all gathering at the Seaways for some big family occasion. Everybody was in process of arriving. I had gone with my parents, and shortly afterwards, Yvonne and Eric turned up. Betty and Bill were there, also Joyce and my late Uncle Len. Nelly was there, but not her husband or any of her children for some reason, although my cousins, Gary and Terry, the sons of my Auntie Joyce, were both present with their girlfriends, Kaz and Trish. Grandpa Stan's best mate, Reg, was there, and as I sat in the downstairs dining room with other members of the family, Reg came in and spoke to me.

"Come with me, Ian! Your Grandpa Stan wants you, and your Uncle Sid! He's got something to tell you!"

We walked from the dining room with the eyes of everyone else in the room fixed upon us. I knew that as soon as the door closed the hubbub would begin as to why I had been singled out and what Grandpa Stan could possibly be planning now. I felt a thrill of excitement as Uncle Reg, as I had come to know him, led me upstairs to the room that Grandpa Stan called his 'study'. I walked into the room, which was full of smoke, and there I found Uncle Sid and Grandpa Stan waiting for me.

"Aw gud!" said Grandpa Stan. "Giv 'im a drink, Reg, an' yo' sit dahn, mate. That's it! Nah, please dun't interrupt me for the next few minutes 'cos I've got summat to tell yer. I can't die 'appy until I've told yer, so pin back yer lugholes and listen!"

I sat down next to Uncle Sid, who was smoking and drinking a large Scotch and ginger. Reg handed me a drink, and I took a good long swig. Grandpa Stan shuffled his feet then he began to speak. Just as he did so, however, the door to his 'study' flew open and my mam and my Grannie Annie were there in the room.

"Cum on, Stan!" said Grannie Annie. "They'll all be here in a tick, an' you're still sittin' in 'ere wivv your feet up an' in your old togs! Cum on, mate, make haste, eh?"

My mam took hold of my hand to guide me out of the room and tut-tutted over the large drink I had been consuming, and at that moment I woke up from that very strange and rather frustrating dream. Now I would never discover what it was my late Grandpa Stan had been about to divulge, and it would be a source of considerable aggravation to me for some time in the future.

I wondered if the dream was an omen. Perhaps they were telling me that by and large, things would be okay, even if we had a rocky road to travel, maybe it would all turn out right in the end. Please, someone up there, please make it all turn out right in the end!

❧❧

I finished my chores and then collapsed onto the sofa with a large mug of tea and a plate heaped with buttered toast and two hard-boiled eggs. I would enjoy a good breakfast before preparing for the inevitable; the big shop and then the 'homecoming'. I was still feeling very apprehensive, but I had to try to quell those feelings of anxiety, or they would show and Andy would realise how unsure I was about having him home. Above all else, I did not want him to guess how I was really feeling. I wanted his homecoming to be a joyous and pleasant occasion, and I would do my ultimate best to see that it was so, even if it killed me!

As I finished my breakfast, the phone rang. I stood up and silenced its insistent clamouring.

"Hello!" I said into the receiver.

"Boyzie! It's Little Dot, Andy's mom!"

We had not spoken for some time, but I had always had a place in my heart for Andy's mom, who was a lively character, always ready with a smile and a kind word whenever she met me. She thought the world of me, but was very concerned about my decision to have Andy to live with me in Milling Street. Having said all that, however, the lady had never offered to have him to live at their house - his home for years - so I was a little taken aback to hear her voice at the other end of the phone that morning.

"Oh! Hello Dot! What cooks?"

"I am baking actually!" she told me. "I thought I'd make you a pie for later on. I know Pam and Pauline are coming in to clean for you while you are at the hospital, and Terry said he would bring me over 'cos I've got a load o' stuff to bring. I'm… I'm sorry as how I haven't bin in touch with you for a while, luv, but… well… you know… I have been thinking abaht you, Boyzie!"

"I know!" I said. "It's good of you to want to make pies and all, and I thank you for it, luv! Yes! There's plenty of room in the pantry and the two freezers, and I'll be delighted to see you and any of the gang later on today, you know that without asking, at least

I hope so anyway."

"Aw gud!" said Dot, reverting to her strong North Midland accent. "So, we'll all see you later on, an' I knaw everything is going to be fine when you see 'im later on today, so dun't worry, eh luv?"

"I'll try not to let it get to me, but... well... I do so want everything to be okay. I've planned everything so meticulously, and... well... I couldn't bear it if it all went wrong at this late stage in the game, know what I mean, Dot?"

I could almost hear the smile in her voice as she continued.

"Dun't yo' fret luv! He's so lucky to have a friend like you, an' in his heart he knaws it an' all."

We said our goodbyes and she told me she would see me later on when I returned from the hospital with Andy. I poured myself another cuppa and sat down to drink it before going back upstairs to make the bed etc.

Yes! Maybe by now he did realise how lucky he was to have a friend like me, but it had not always been so. Oh no! In the past... I had to stop thinking of the past! That was a time gone by. Now the future beckoned, such as it was, and we had to all knuckle down and endeavour to make the best of it, whatever it might hold for all of us. With that thought uppermost in my mind, I went off upstairs to make the bed, finish preparing for my outing and to try and calm myself prior to what was to come later on that momentous day!

❦

Bob Douse duly arrived and he drove me to Allerton. I undertook a big shop and met lots of people with whom I chatted easily as I travelled around the various establishments in order to make my purchases. As usual, Allerton was bursting with people. Saturday was always a busy day in that part of Gaynsford. I think people came out as much for the society of others as to undertake shopping etc., because everywhere you went, people were laughing, chatting, arguing, generally getting together for one reason or another.

That afternoon there would be football, and our glorious team was playing at home. Our glory days were not as glorious as once they had been, but we still gave a pretty good account of ourselves. The team manager those days was Les Greaves, little Les Greaves who had scored the vital goals that had clinched the FA Challenge Cup for us all those years before, back in the late seventies - a momentous day indeed, still remembered by many residents of Gaynsford.

I made all my purchases, including a brand new radio-cassette player and a new portable TV for Andy's room, and we decided to take both of them along with us that afternoon instead of waiting for them to be delivered. We made four journeys to and from Bob's cab, but he only had the meter on for the journeys to and from Osleston, the rest of the money I had agreed with him prior to his arrival that morning.

Bob had left his wife, Carol, who had the custody of Steven and Joni, plus the other two children they had had. Bob lived with a woman called Sandra, who had several sons, and I guess he was happy enough, but his former wife had been a good sort and I had been very sorry when I knew they were splitting up. The children had never really become acclimatised to their parents' separation, and Steven had become very disturbed. There was talk that he was going to move back to live with Bob and his lady friend, but as I say, they had quite a houseful already, and it was rumoured that she was pregnant by Bob, although he had never confirmed that to me. I would not ask, even though we had known each other for many years. If Bob wanted me to know the details of his family life then he would relay those to me in person.

We drove home to Milling Street and found the house running alive with people! Half of Andy's family seemed to be there! Bob helped me in with all the shopping, and Andy's mom and sisters, Pam, Pauline and Shirley, said they would put everything away and put out all the things I desired, to be ready for when Andy came home. His brothers, Terry and Lennie, said they would rig up the radio and the TV ready for him, and all in all the situation appeared to have been taken out of my hands completely.

I was given a cuppa, as was Bob, before we left at around 12.15 p.m. to go to the hospital to fetch Andy home to Osleston. I was shaking! I know it was silly, but I really was shaking!

16

Monday, 19th November 1990.

I PUT OUT my hand to silence the persistent ringing of the alarm clock that stood on the bedside table to the left of me. I had just enjoyed the best night's sleep I had had since Andy had come home to live with me, just over a fortnight before, and I awoke that morning feeling thoroughly refreshed and ready for almost anything! I felt great! I sat myself up in the bed and thrust my legs right down to the bottom. I felt so warm and comfortable, and so refreshed! I really felt as though life was taking a turn for the better - at last. Things had gone so much better than I had believed, no, far better than I had dared to hope.

When Andy had first returned home, he was very clinging; he wanted me to sit beside his bed when he went to sleep at night, as though he was a child. He did not want me in one bedroom and him in another, no, he wanted me to sleep in the chair in his room or else sleep on the bed, or at least to always be there in some way so that if he awoke in the night and needed reassurance, he would know I was there to give it.

When I thought of how he used to be prior to that dreadful night in April of that year, I found it very difficult to believe that the guy who now lived with me was the same one who had used me so savagely and cruelly. That bloke had been so strong, so sure of himself. He had been very self-assured, tough, with a 'devil-may-care' attitude. He had literally swaggered around, very full of his own importance when he was in the mood, but when he was behaving normally there had been no one kinder, no one more caring or thoughtful – no one more considerate.

Well, he now seemed to be a totally different person, most of the time anyway. Very little self-confidence, hardly any glimmer of a sense of humour. Not a lot of life in him! He was, in effect, hard work at times, and yet… and yet I knew I should persevere, that I ought not to just give up on him, in fact I knew I could never do that. No! We had come too far for me to just give up on him. I suppose the thing that kept me going was the occasional 'good' day, or perhaps when something pleased him and he seemed happy, contented for a brief moment in time, or, even better, when he actually laughed at something I might have said or even at something he might have said. That was when I saw glimpses of the old Andy coming through, and I felt that perhaps all my efforts were not entirely in vain, but for most of the time it was very hard work!

Not to put too fine a point on it, I was getting tired. My job was ever more demanding, as my case load increased. I was kept very busy from the time I arrived until the time I left most days, and then when I got home I had a good deal to do around the house, besides the personal care I had to give to Andy. Of course, his family was very good, and also I had help from carers; professionals who came in regularly four times a week to help him to bathe, shave and take physical exercise, walking around, out of his wheelchair.

At night, after our meal, when I had tidied around, washed up the pots etc., I usually sat with him, listening to music, watching TV or else I read to him. Most of the time, he dozed as I did those things, but sometimes, depending on the amount of pills he had taken, he could be quite lively company and, indeed, could become quite chatty and, on the odd occasion, actually quite lively! I used to endeavour to quell that initial excitement, but then I was happy whenever he became animated, as long as I knew it would not result in a fit of any kind, a bout of hysteria or some other extreme mode of behaviour. At least, if he showed some semblance of activity, it proved he was 'alive'. Oh! Don't misunderstand! I was not sorry I had him back home to live with me, at least not then anyway, but as I have already intimated, sometimes it just felt like all the pressure was on me and I found it hard to take it all on my shoulders. With the demands of my job and all, I didn't need all that hassle at home as well.

I lay in bed for a few moments longer prior to getting up and preparing to start yet another busy day. Once out of bed, I found my socks, put them on and then stood to open the window. I then made the bed. Andy's sister, Eileen, would be coming in tomorrow, and she would take any clothes, bed-linen etc., to the laundry for me. She would wait while it is washed and spun dry then she would come back with it and she and her husband, Ron, would take me shopping.

I had a couple of days off that week - Tuesday and Wednesday - and I was basically looking forward to the break. The weather at present was quite fine, although rather chilly. Still, after we had been shopping, and Andy and I had had some dinner in the early afternoon, we might go down to the park if he felt up to it. I enjoyed pushing him in his wheelchair in the park, and if he was in a good mood we had quite a laugh while he 'helped' me by telling me, 'Right here. Oyshie!' or 'Left a few yards along 'ere, Oyshie!'. He 'led' me around the paths that criss-crossed the park, and we usually thoroughly enjoyed our visits there, especially when the kids were still at school and there were not too many people around. Andy used to get very embarrassed about sitting in his wheelchair while I pushed him, but soon he did not worry about it so much. He merely enjoyed the idea of getting out of the house for a while, no matter how that was achieved. We used to find somewhere to sit for a while after I had pushed him up and down the various paths around the park, and then, if we felt like it, we would have a drink. I usually took a flask with us, and maybe I would read a while, either to him or to myself while he sat and looked around, enjoying the freedom and the fresh air.

I knew he got thoroughly bored at times, but I tried very hard to fill his time as much as I was able. There was talk among the professionals that he might be able to go to a day centre three or four days per week, if he wanted to do so and if I agreed, so that he could get some stimulation, although the last social worker, Jim Hunter, who visited me, had said he reckoned I provided plenty of stimulation for Andy!

Of course, I constantly encouraged him to broaden his horizons. I tried almost daily to set him goals to achieve in the hope that, by achieving them, even if they were simple, it might well give him the incentive and motivation to go farther, and endeavour to break down barriers in order to achieve even more. More often than not, it did seem to work, however, that morning Andy was in a truculent mood. He had not slept particularly well, and did not want to get up. When I eventually persuaded him to get up and partially dress himself - to put on his socks and his lower garments - he just sat on the edge of the bed swinging his legs, making no attempt to finish dressing, or to make an effort to go to the bathroom to wash.

I was busy getting my breakfast and making coffee for both of us when he suddenly called out.

"Oyshie!"

His speech was still rather slurred, and often he could not say my nickname correctly.

"Well?" I said, returning to sit on the bed beside him.

He had his head down resting on his arms, and I put my arms around his shoulders. He was sobbing.

"Hey! What's up, big fella?" I asked.

It was a while before he could answer me, and when he did, I had quite a shock.

"I wanna work, Oyshie!" he said brokenly.

We sat together for a while, me with my arm around his shaking shoulders. I had left milk boiling on the stove and bread under the grill, so I had to move. When I returned to his bedroom, he had managed to finish dressing, after a fashion, and I helped him to tidy himself up before he sat down and I gave him his breakfast. As he ate, he spoke again.

"I wanna work, Oyshie! I'm goin' barmy stuck in 'ere all the time. I wanna 'av summat te do wot will stimulate me, an' mek' me feel useful again, you know, Oyshie! You know!"

Of course I did know, and I empathised, but I was unsure how I was supposed to help him in that regard.

"What about this day centre idea they keep on about?" I said, being careful, anxious not to antagonise or upset him.

"Naw! That's not wot I want at all. I want te do summat useful, like when I was workin' for the police back then. Surely there's summat I could do that's stimulatin' an' worthwhile. Surely I dun't 'av te spend the rest of my life..."

He burst into a flood of tears once more, and again I sat beside him while his bout of near hysteria subsided. I felt helpless for almost the first time since he had arrived home. I was completely out of my depth and did not know how best to go about helping him in the way he required and desired. I vowed to phone Jim Hunter as soon as possible when I got to the office to see whether two heads might be better than one in that situation. In the meantime, I had to get ready for work and had to try to encourage my charge to finish his breakfast and complete his preparations for the remainder of the morning, prior to my leaving him for several hours. I made a mental note to try and get home for lunchtime, so I could be with him, but I would just take it steady that morning. After all, I could not rush him, not when he was so upset. That would not be kind. No! That morning I would just have to move along steadily and go at Andy's pace.

As a consequence of our slow pace that morning, I was late into the office and for a vital team meeting. I had a new 'gaffer' then. Jeremiah Johnson had left us and we had two new senior councillors, as Shirley Beresford had also left. Our new team leader was Sally Kelly, and she was assisted by Richard Proctor. Sal and Dick were both okay, but they were both workaholics, and they desired that the members of their team were also motivated and in 'work mode' the same as themselves. I had never given either of them cause for concern, at least not knowingly anyway, but neither of them smiled fondly on anyone who was late for meetings! Unless one had a cast iron reason for not attending, regular involvement in meetings was of paramount importance, especially to Sally Kelly, and non-attendance was punishable on pain of death!

Both Sally and Richard knew all about my home circumstances. I think Richard, who was married with three young children, first thought I was gay when he heard of my situation, but Mike Groves, Wayne Clarke and myself, plus others, quickly disabused him of that thought! Sally Kelly expressed her heartfelt sympathy, but said that she hoped it would not impinge too greatly upon my work as a counsellor, knowing how very busy we were etc., etc. I bristled a little at that, saying quite loudly and forcefully that at no time in the past had it ever interfered with my work within the Family Support Centre, and I went on to say that even when my late wife was so very ill, I still attended and worked to the very best of my capabilities. Sally smiled sweetly and said she was pleased to hear that, and hoped it would continue, at which point, I tactfully withdrew from the interview, fearing that if I stayed any longer in her presence, I just might be tempted to carry out a physical assault upon her person, which would have benefited no one! How very different from the attitude of the lovely Pat Lenham, who had always been so kind and considerate, so caring and compassionate whenever anyone had problems at home or in any other respect pertaining to their families.

Sally was 28 years of age. She had come up on the 'fast track' and she was single. Rumour had it that she had a fella, but the joke was that he had no balls 'cos she had eaten 'em! Knowing the lioness she purported to be, that did not surprise.

When I arrived at the office that morning, however, Sally was all sweetness and light.

"Hello, Boyzie! Everything okay, love?"

I said it was, but I think she could tell by my demeanour that I was lying.

"Do you want to talk about it at all? Is it Andy again?"

I nodded my head.

"Come into my office and have a cuppa with me, then I can fill you in on what we discussed at the meeting this morning," she said.

I told her I was up to my neck in work and had an interview at around 11 a.m., but she said it did not matter. What they had discussed that morning would be of interest to me, and she wished to impart information to me as a team member, therefore, I had little choice but to obey the command. We both sat down in Sally's office and she immediately became conspiratorial.

"Now then, Boyzie, what's it all about, love?"

I felt I had been trapped into the situation and was not best pleased. However, her attitude was ultimately preferable to that which I had initially expected, so I should not really complain. Instead, I imparted to her the information that Andy was becoming restless and wished to undertake some kind of work again in the near future. Sally ordered us more coffee and called Richard Proctor and also Mike Groves and Chris Braun to see if they were all able to be present for a general discussion. I was very surprised and tried to protest, but my protest was knocked back.

"I may have a solution to his problem, and yours," said Sally, with great confidence.

Oh, well then! Maybe we should all have a chat, if it might ultimately lead to the end of some of Andy's difficulties and the feeling he had that he was jockin' useless. Mike, Chris and Wayne Clarke all duly arrived in the office and after a few moments Richard Proctor made an appearance as well. A full-blown meeting between me and the entire senior management team at the Family Support Centre.

At the culmination of that meeting, which lasted well over an hour, it was felt we might have the framework of a strategy to enable Andy to get restarted back on the road to a fuller and more active life! The plan we had formulated was as follows. Joy Farnesworth, who had been the receptionist-cum-switchboard operator for about nine months, was going off on maternity leave, but the day before she had told Mike and Chris that she did not intend to return, thus, they would be looking for a replacement.

Did I think Andy would be interested? Furthermore, did I and the medical staff caring for him believe he would be up to the job? It was very demanding and the switchboard, and indeed the reception area, could become very busy and extremely noisy and congested at times. How did we feel? Did I believe there would be sufficient access into the building for Andy with his wheelchair? If not, then maybe if he decided he wanted the job and we decided to employ him, we could get a council grant to have the whole of the reception area and the foyer of the building revamped to allow good access for Andy into and out of the building.

I said I would talk to Doctor Braden at the hospital and also to Doctor Jarvis at our local practice to see what they would both say, but that personally I thought it was a superb idea, and I felt that Andy would be capable of taking on the duties, and further that he would want to do so, and with gusto. I could not wait to get home that evening to tell him what we had been discussing and outlining for him, and how I believed such a move would benefit him and afford him a new lease of life!

The other exciting event that occurred that day took place at around lunchtime. I was just about to go out to the Gunners for a ploughman's lunch with Chris, Wayne and Otis Masher when the phone rang. Joy informed me that it was someone called Mike Milan from the Guide Dogs for the Blind Association. Oh good! I had not heard from them for a long time, in fact, I had begun to believe they had forgotten all about me, but no! Mike Milan sounded pleasant enough.

"Is that Mr Ian Dickson?" he asked.

"Speaking!" I responded.

Mike then went on to introduce himself and to tell me that he hoped they might have matched me up with a suitable dog. I was so taken aback that I stuttered!

"O-oh! Well… er… I-I still want one, you know!"

He laughed.

"Aw! Good!" he said. "I think you will be pleased with the one we have for you. I wanted to talk to you about the arrangements for training with your new dog!"

I could still not quite believe it. After all that time! I was to have a guide dog, and it really was not very convenient then, but I could hardly turn it down. Suppose I never got another opportunity? I would rue the day I turned down the chance to train with my new guide dog, and I knew that, if I were to ask him, or indeed if he were there beside me, Andy would tell me to 'go for it'. So perhaps I had better do exactly that! In fairness to my mate, Andy, I ought to endeavour to explain to Mike Milan the circumstances pertaining, and the reasons why it would be difficult for me to undertake training away from home at that time.

I began to tell my story, and very soon I knew that Mike Milan was listening intently and that he would, if possible, attempt to find a suitable solution to my predicament. By the time I had put the receiver back on its rest, we had more or less resolved the situation. I would be trained at home, so that I could still afford good care to Andy. Mike Milan would speak to his senior training adviser and the centre manager, and would ask for a period of up to five weeks during which he would be domiciled up there in Gaynsford, North Midlands, and he would visit me daily to work with me. We would undertake a variety of routes that I used regularly, find some quiet walks we could undertake to give the dog a little rest and relaxation. We would work on traffic, crossing and recrossing roads, travel on public transport, buses, trains etc., visit the shops, pub, church, and local schools in the immediate vicinity of where I lived, then move into the town, and later on into the city centre. We would assess the dog at all levels of the work we would undertake, and Mike would make a weekly report of how we were doing, and endeavour to maintain both my progress and that of the dog during our training sessions.

Qualification would hopefully come at the end of say, five weeks, when Mike was sure I had learned and absorbed everything he had been able to impart to me, and also when he had ensured that the dog was absolutely in tune with me and that we were working together as a well-organised and successful partnership. He told me the dog he had in mind for me was female, that she was a black labrador, aged 19 months, she was quite small, but very lively, sturdy, well balanced socially and a good little worker. Her name was Pepsi! He told me he would be bringing her up to meet me on Friday, 11th January 1991, and that he would leave her with me over the weekend so we could get used to one another. On the morning of Monday, 14th January 1991, my training with Pepsi would commence. Heck! What a day that was turning out to be, and it was still only lunchtime yet!

I had intended to go out to lunch with Chris, but at the last minute he couldn't make it - some big meeting or other. He apologised for having to let me down, but as it transpired, I was not too concerned. I could go home and have my lunch hour with Andy. I would be able to impart the information to him about the discussions we had had during the morning, and put to him the idea we had formulated, to see if he approved.

੪ೱ੨

I left the Family Support Centre and caught a bus to Osleston. The day was fine. I got off the bus at my usual stop in high spirits, and commenced the walk home to Milling Street. As I turned left onto Fletcher Street, the one before Milling Street, I heard a siren; loud, urgent. An ambulance went by at an alarming speed! Oh God! I wondered who that was for. It sure seemed urgent! I walked on towards my house, my heart singing. Perhaps we were really getting somewhere at last. If we could help to rehabilitate Andy by getting him settled in a job that he enjoyed, that would be a great boost.

I thought of the three visually impaired guys, Phil Mackie, Graham Roddis and Steve Gregson, who had now arrived in Africa to endeavour to fulfil their ambitions to climb Mount Kilimanjaro. The newspapers, the media etc., had been full of it, and the money was apparently pouring in for their chosen charity; the cure for river blindness out on the African Continent. Perhaps Andy and I were also on the verge of completing our ascent of Mount Kilimanjaro? I hoped so. I hoped so very much indeed!

I had reached the corner of Fletcher and Milling, and there seemed to be a great many people out in our street that lunchtime. Several of the neighbours came running down to meet me.

"Oh! Oh, Boyzie! Thank goodness you are here!"

My heart sank down into my boots. Oh my God! What had happened now? I was met at my front gate by a number of people including three of Andy's sisters, Eileen, Pam and Paula, and his mom, Little Dot, who threw her arms around my neck and buried her face in my shoulder.

"He's gone, Boyzie, he's gone!" she wailed, as she shook with sobs.

I could not move or speak. A hand landed on my shoulder and I half-turned. Andy Lee, the paramedic, was standing behind me.

"We're tekin' 'im into the County Hospital," he told me. "He's had a massive grand mal and he's unconscious."

Apparently Andy had suffered a category one epileptic fit about an hour and a half after I had left him. His three sisters were at the house and his mom had just arrived as it occurred, so they had all witnessed it.

"Who's going with him?" I asked, my voice shaking.

"Me," said his mom, raising her tear-stained face from my wet shoulder. "An - an' yo' oughta cum too, my luv. He'd want yo' te cum!"

I spoke briefly to his sisters, who told me they would ensure that the house was secure etc., before they went home, and then I was climbing into the ambulance with Little Dot, and asking my next-door neighbour, Sharon, if she would kindly phone my office for me and also if she would please ring Father Martyn and ask him to call me or to come down to the hospital to be with us. Sharon, who was a lovely woman, mother of a large clan of unruly kids, and a battered wife, although he no longer lived with the family, said she would do that for me, and the ambulance sped on its way once we were all aboard, the siren blaring out its urgent call!

Off to the County Hospital *again*! Oh! Would it never end?

17

Thursday, 6th December.

I T WAS less than three weeks until Christmas Day, and I could not have cared less about Christmas, or anything remotely connected with its celebrations!

At 10.50 a.m. I was seated in the front of the first of four black limousines, following the hearse towards Saint Peter and Saint Paul's Roman Catholic Church in Town End, the part of Gaynsford in which most of Andy's large and very close-knit family resided. That was where he had been brought up, that was the part of town that he had always considered as home.

The cortege moved very slowly through the streets towards its destination. The neighbours were out in force; all of them out in the streets, dressed in their best, there to say their last goodbyes to him. He and his family must have been, indeed must still be, very popular around there. It was good to realise so many people cared, and it would be a comfort to his family to see so many people whom they knew had come out to say their last farewell to a 'son' of the area.

How proud his mom must have felt. She was in the back of the vehicle, along with her son, Lennie, and two of her daughters - the two eldest. I was in the front of the limousine, along with his two elder brothers, Bernie and Terry, and the driver. We had hired four, big black limousines to follow the hearse carrying him to his last resting-place. Well, not quite his last. After the Mass at Saint

Peter and Saint Paul's, we would drive, the family that is and a few chosen friends, over to the crematorium and hold a brief service there, before adjourning to the Gunners, where they were laying on a big buffet lunch to celebrate his life, to which anyone who cared to come was welcome!

I knew the place would be packed out, stacked out with people all wishing to pay their last respects to him! I also knew that at the Gunners they would pull out all the stops to make it a great occasion. That was what we had asked for. Not a sombre occasion, not a great deal of wallowing in self-pity and misery. No! He would not have wanted that at any cost! He would have wanted the type of celebration that his family and I had planned. His mom was not all together sold on the idea, not initially anyway, but when she realised how keen I was she eventually acquiesced, and became involved in the preparations.

Once the funeral and all its pomp and ceremony was over then the feasting and fun would begin, but as I sat in the limousine, still making its slow and laborious progress towards the church, I did not feel very much like celebrating. As far as I was concerned, they could take Christmas and all its celebrations and sink them down to the bottom of the sea for me that year. I did my best to bear up bravely - after all, I knew that was what he would expect me to do, and no less - but it was hard, bloody hard!

I could hear his mom and sisters quietly talking through the partition that had been drawn over between the front and rear of the vehicle, to give some privacy to those who travelled in the back. His poor mom had been almost inconsolable since the day of his decease, but now she was endeavouring to put a brave face on it, like all the rest of us who had been so deeply affected by his passing. I hung my head as emotion welled up inside me and my eyes filled up with unshed tears. I bit my lip furiously. No, I would not cry! I would not let myself down. Since his decease, I had not cried - well, not in the presence of anyone else anyway - and I would not do so now!

"Nearly there nah!" said Bernie.

A light snow was falling, and had been for several hours. The ground was now covered and the sky was full of the threat of a great deal more to come. Dark clouds hung over everything. That corresponded well with the general mood, but we had to try to lift that mood once the funeral ceremonies were over, because we had all made a promise, a silent promise, but a promise nonetheless, that his wake would be a joyful occasion, one of looking forward in joy rather than looking back in sorrow!

The hearse was turning into the churchyard, which already seemed to be packed with people waiting for the funeral to commence. We followed in the first of the four cars, the other three close on our tail. The other vehicles parked up outside on the road. It was by now after 11 a.m., and the Mass incorporating the funeral service was due to commence at 11.20 a.m. precisely. Our car stopped behind the hearse, and we all alighted from the vehicle with help from the chauffeur. I stood with my arm around the shoulders of Little Dot, my late friend's mother, who was doing her best to keep her spirits up for the occasion to come.

The coffin was being wheeled out of the hearse and flowers were being placed on the top. Andy's mom's and those of the family took precedence, but I had bought a big bouquet as well, and that was well bound and placed with the others of the family, discretely behind those of his mom, sisters and brothers. With my flowers was a large, although not ostentatious, card, which simply read:

Andy!
Good night and God bless. See you in the morning.
Oyshie!

The snow was falling more heavily now as even more people arrived, and the family was congregating together near the doorway leading into the church. People were talking in hushed voices, and it seemed no one could really believe what had occurred, but it *had* occurred. Now he was at rest. No more sorrow, no more suffering. He was at peace at last, and I was free!

I felt bad even thinking like that, albeit I was the only one who knew my innermost thoughts, but I still felt bad about feeling that way. Why should I feel bad? For jock's sake, I had given him everything! I had been to visit him while he had been lying in the hospital those last few days. I had been sitting with him on Thursday, during the mid-afternoon, when he had regained consciousness and seemed to rally. Yes! I had been on my own with him during that time, and that period of time, those couple of hours we had spent together, talking, remembering, me holding tight onto his hand as it lay on the top of the bed, then the last embrace we had shared together - those were memories I would always cherish, and they would be forever unsullied, totally mine, never to be shared with anyone because they were wholly unique to him and me!

I had been sitting beside his bed from around 10 a.m., when his mother and two of his sisters had gone home after keeping an all-night vigil. He had never moved all night, according to Little Dot. She and her two daughters had left the hospital saying they would be back later, but in fact, they had never returned and had not seen him alive again, and neither had any other member of his family. Nobody was with him when he died, it had happened quietly. As he slept soundly and peacefully he had merely relapsed once more into unconsciousness, and then into a deep comatose state, but I had been with him when he had rallied. That had been a wonderful time, a happy time that would always remain with me. I had been talking to him quietly, holding onto his hand, when suddenly he had moved in the bed. He had rolled over, taken my hand in both of his, and as he lay on his back, his eyes flickering open, he must have recognised me. As clearly as he had ever spoken my name, he had said:

"Hi there, Boyzie! How's it hanging, mate?"

It had been such a wonderful surprise to hear him that I could not speak for a moment or two then I pulled myself together.

"Aw! Awake are you? Ready for something to eat and drink I'll be bound!"

He had waited a moment before responding.

"Naw! Aw dunna want owt to eat, but aw cud drink a jockin' well dry, Boyzie!"

I had smiled to myself and called the nurse over. She filled a big jug with ice-cold water and we propped him up against five pillows, so he could drink. I reached for the brimming glass, gave it to him, and his hands trembled as he took it. He drank steadily.

"Aw! Fanks, Oyshie!" he said, slipping almost subconsciously into the slow, drawling way he had recently acquired when speaking. "That was gud, mate!"

I took the glass and placed it on his bedside table, then helped him to lie back and made him as comfortable as I could. I took his hand again and we sat quietly for a while.

"Oyshie?"

I squeezed his hand gently.

"Well?" I said, giving it yet another gentle squeeze to encourage him to speak to me.

"Aw'm… aw'm heart sorry for wot aw done to you, mate! Aw… aw never meant te hurt yo', Oyshie! Aw… aw… well, aw luv yo' like a bruvver, mate, an' aw wud never 'av done anyfink te hurt yo', but… but well… aw… aw jus' lost it… yo' knaw wot I mean, eh Oyshie?" He was quiet for a few moments then he continued. "Arter aw had done wot aw done, aw went into your bedroom-"

I gently interrupted him with yet another squeeze of his big hand.

"Look, mate, you don't have to tell me all this now. It's all in the past and…"

"Naw! Let me tell yo' 'cos I want yo' te knaw wot happened!"

I resigned myself to listening to whatever he had to say, but hoped that when he had finished, it would not have taken too much out of him, either physically or emotionally.

"Okay, Andy. I won't interrupt any more. Go on and tell me what you want to say, and I promise I'll listen!"

It took him a moment or two to rally his thoughts then he began.

"Aw was hurt when yo' spoke te me the way yo' did that afternoon, Oyshie, so that's why I lashed aht at yo' in the kitchen! When yo' were lyin' on the bed, an' aw went into the room an' sat dahn beside yer, well, aw jus' wanted te be friends again an' aal. Yo' wudna' 'av it, wud yo', mate? Aw suppose aw shud 'av understud how yo' was feelin', but… well, aw jus' felt bluddy angry that yo' wudn't be friends wiv me, so… so aw started drinkin'. When aw was feelin' pretty bluddy, an' well oiled, aw rushed into the shower an'… well… yo' knaw wot happened then, dun't yo', my mate?"

I still retained hold of his hand. I shivered at the memory his words evoked.

"Yes, I know. Go on Andy."

"Giv us another drink please, mate!" he said, and I once more gave him the brimming glass of water, still cold.

He sipped from the glass before I replaced it again and once more sat down, taking his hand in both of mine and giving it an affectionate squeeze. He relaxed, and began to talk again.

"Aw was a bluddy fool! Aw shudna 'av treated yo', my bes' mate, like that, but… well… somehow, once aw started te kick an' punch yo' well, aw jus' lost control o' my emotions, an' aw cudn't stop. Can yo' understand that, Oyshie? Can yo', my mate?"

I was feeling very emotional, but I could not shed tears then, not when he was so deeply engrossed in what he was telling me.

"Yes! Yes, I think so," I said, hoping he would not ask me to go on and explain, because I did not think I could manage to do so without bursting into tears.

"Aw gud!" he said with feeling. "Aw knaw 'ow much I hurt yo' an… an' aw'm heart sorry for it, mate. Aw'd do anyfink te turn the clock back, an' mek' it all go away, but… well… aw can't do that, can I, mate?"

I remembered lying flat on the floor of the shower at Depot Street, while he sprawled across me, singing loudly and raucously, 'Here we go, here we go here we go! Here we go, here we go, here we go-o'. I found it hard to think about those events of the past and to feel forgiveness in my heart for the way he had treated me, but I did admire his honesty and realised as he continued to talk to me, just what it was costing him emotionally to tell me how he had felt on that dreadful night.

"When aw had finished kickin' an' punchin' yo' abaht, an' arter aw stud uvver yo' an'… an' done wot aw done te yo', then aw went back into your bedroom an' aw sprawled naked on your bed. Aw became more an' more drunk, an' eventually aw began to hate myself for wot aw'd done te yo', an' then I felt very guilty!"

Suddenly his whole body had been racked with a fit of coughing, and I held him in my arms until the fit passed over him! As I laid him back down against the pillows piled up behind him, I begged him gently to rest, but he was determined to get to the end of his narrative.

"Naw, Oyshie! Lemmee finish wot aw've got te say, then aw con relax. It's playin' on my mind, mate, an' aw wanna tell yo' it aal!"

His accent was becoming more and more pronounced, and I could tell how tired he was because his words were slurring together more and more as he spoke.

"It's all right, Andy, I'm listening."

He waited a while before he recommenced speaking.

"Do yo' remember that mornin', Boyzie, the mornin' yo' 'ad your interview for the position as counsellor at the Family Support Centre?"

"Well?" I queried again.

He asked for a drink, and after he had partaken of the refreshing liquid, he lay back again then proceeded to continue.

"Aw was readin' to yo', remember? Abaht those three lads yo' knew at school, remember, mate?"

I remembered. I gave his big hand a reassuring squeeze.

"Yes!" I managed. "Yes, I remember!"

"They are goin' te climb that big mountain aht in Africa, ain't they, Boyzie?" he said.

I nodded - I could not speak. He continued slowly, his speech becoming quite slurred as he grew more and more tired.

"Yo' reckoned as 'ow wae cud climb a big mountain togevver! We tried hard, didn't we, mate?"

I hung my head, and the tears cascaded hot from my swollen eyes.

"Oh! Oh, Andy!" I said, and embraced him hard.

I sat with my arm around his shoulders as he continued.

"We're almost there, aren't we, mate? We're almost at the summit of ahr own mountain, aren't we, Oyshie?"

I could not speak for a few moments then as I laid him down, making him as comfortable as I possibly could, he said:

"We're pretty near the top of ahr own mountain, ain't we, my mate?"

I managed to reply.

"Yes! Yes, Andy, we are almost there now!"

"Gud!" he said, and he sighed. "Aw fink aw'll try an' 'av a little rest nah, Oyshie!" he told me.

"Yes! Yes, you do that, mate, and I'll stay quietly by you while you do... if that's okay?" I added as an afterthought.

"Dun't yo' dare go away!" he said, and he moved to put an arm around me. "Aw luv yo', mate! Aw luv yo' like a bruvver!"

Those were the last words Andy Gange ever said to me!

§⇒⊷§

It was 1.45 p.m. and the ceremonials and the Mass were all over. We were driving to the Gunners for the wake. Andy had finally been laid to rest, and now, life had to continue, for me and for all members of his family, but how? How would I continue to get through life without him? I had made so many adjustments. I had put my life more or less on hold so that I could continue to care for my best, my dearest mate!

I could not forget the talk we had had prior to his decease. How honest he had been. How he had declared to me his heartfelt sorrow at all he had done to me, and, of course, I believed him! Why the jockin' hell should I not? You may think I believed him because I wanted to believe he had never meant to hurt me. Well, that is wrong. On that night - that dreadful night in April when it had all begun to go pear-shaped - I was sure he meant to hurt me, and frankly, as his behaviour towards me grew more and more bizarre, I really started to fear for my life. No! I was under no illusions! When he was drunk and doing the things he had done to me on that terrible and never-to-be-forgotten night in April, I was sure he had meant everything he was doing and that he had intended to hurt me and maybe even kill me! To have heard his honest appraisal of what had occurred was a complete revelation to me. It was good to know how he felt about it all and that he had never meant to behave like that towards me - it was all fuelled by anger, frustration and petty jealousy, and later by booze! Yes! I honestly believed his appraisal of what had occurred had been entirely honest, and that he was easing his own conscience prior to dying when he told me all that as he lay there in the bed beside which I sat, holding on tightly to his big hand.

Like he had said to me, I also had loved him! Like a brother? I did not know how to assess fully and completely my feelings for Andy, not at that time, anyway. That came later! Much later on, and when it did finally come to me, how I had really felt about him, it came as something of a shock! Now I am rushing on again! One step at a time, Boyzie, one step at a time!

18

I T WAS the second day of a New Year! I was up in Harts Hill, and had spent Christmas with my sister, Doreen, and her husband, Fred.

On Christmas Day, the whole family had been together at Ploughman's Cottage, and it was total and utter chaos, but it was all truly wonderful nonetheless. So many people; all the grandchildren, all the kids together, and young Eric positively blossoming! He had been so delighted to see me when I had arrived, and he had practically never left my side since then. He had even insisted on coming with Fred to meet me! Eric was a smashing kid. Even though he had Down's syndrome, he had a great sense of humour, he was a 'clown' and loved to fool around. He made me and everyone else fall about with laughter most of the time.

Muriel was home. She was a sullen girl, but seemed to be more well adjusted those days. At least she was much more accepting of Eric and his presence within the family. At one time, she had been very resentful of him and almost hated him, or so it seemed at any rate, but at times she was almost protective of him now, not that he needed anyone to protect him; he could look after himself very nicely, thank you.

All the other kids were delighted to see me! Five of them were married or had partners. Peggy Sue had married a guy called Jeff. His name was actually Jefferson, and he and his family originally came from South Africa. Peggy Sue and Jeff had a large and bois-terous family, but they were very proud of all of them. Frank was married to a gal called Lena. June's husband was Ben, a big strap-ping lad. Arthur was married to Rita. She was rather loud, and giggled a lot, but she was all right. Ellen, or Nell, had married a lad called Billy. Jack and Fred were still both single, and they worked alongside their dad.

Fred now had charge of over 1,000 pigs and also more than 2,500 chickens, so he was broadening his horizons and was kept extremely busy around the farm those days - much busier than he had ever been in the past. Iris, not wed, had two small chil-dren, a girl called Holly and a boy called Brad. They lived at home with Doreen and Fred. The four younger boys, Gordie, Mal, Den and Trev, all still lived at home too, so the house was still pretty crowded, and the animals just seemed to abound there.

Dorrie was very happy with her large and chaotic family, and she thrived on all the work, the kids, the grandchildren, the friends she had, the fun and the wonderful love she shared with her husband, big Freddie. They were so ideally matched and so wonderfully happy, but their chaotic lifestyle would not have done for me, not permanently anyway, although I did love to visit them in the north-east - but no, I could not live as they did, not for all the rice in China!

Anyway, as I say, Christmas was a tremendous success and a truly happy time for all of us! I needed that tonic; time spent with my family, to get over the decease of Andy Gange. Of course, like all the other people I had lost and loved in my life, I would never properly get over the death of Andy, but at least going to spend Christmas and the New Year up there in Harts Hill had helped me to realise that life had to go on, despite how a person might feel.

It was 2nd January 1991, and I wondered, as I always do at this time of a new year, what the next 364 days would hold for me and mine!

19

AT 4 p.m. on a raw winter afternoon with the wind blowing off the sea and the mists hanging over everything, a
long, sleek black car pulled up at Ploughman's Cottage,
and Eddie and Vinny, two of Norma Townley's sons, got out of
the front of the vehicle and made their way towards the house. As
they knocked at the front door and opened it, I was ready.

That afternoon I was going over to Norma's for tea. She had
called and invited me the day after Boxing Day. She would love to
see me again, she said, and many of her family members would
be at the house, and they would all love to see me as well. That
came as something of a surprise to me. When I had last met up
with Norma and members of her clan, the atmosphere among us
had not been all that great. It was about 18 months before, and
Norma had not seen me for some considerable time, in fact, the
time before was on the occasion of my visit to see Sandy, when
Belle, the child who Sandy was so sure was mine, was still alive,
back in August of 1979.

As I say, I had seen her and some of her family approximately
18 months before when I was up staying with Dorrie and Fred for
a brief period during the early part of the summer, and she had
been almost hostile towards me. Now she wanted to see me, so,
with some reservations, I went along with Eddie, Vinny and their
wives, sitting in the back of the car with the women as we travelled over to Norma's house.

On arrival, I was greeted warmly by Norma, her daughter,

Barbara, Babs's partner plus several of her children, Kenny and Sue and their clan, plus various children of Eddie and Vinny and their consorts plus offspring, and also the younger members of Norma's family. The place was full of people, and once more it was chaos!

"It's grand te see yo', mon!" said Norma. "Sit yo' dahn nah, an' one o' the lasses'l get yo' a drink."

"Thanks," I said, and was guided to a chair, from which four cats quickly jumped and sped off into the disorderly kitchen!

I was almost immediately besieged by Norma's grandchildren, who climbed all over me, eager to share with me their toys, their books etc., etc. They took to me easily and well, and it was lovely! I felt very much at home in the warmth of that totally chaotic, but nevertheless loving, family. I had two large Scotch whiskies with American dry ginger, and then it was time for tea!

Norma had pulled out all the stops. We had ham salad, pork pie, toasted teacakes, stottie cake, scones with strawberry jam and thick clotted cream, sherry trifle, for the adults, which was full of sherry and simply laden with fresh fruit. Afterwards there was coffee and walnut sponge, and Victoria jam sponge! The kids enjoyed a variety of sandwiches, jellies, chocolate mousse etc., etc., and there were plenty of soft drinks for them, and tea or coffee for the adults - a most splendid bill of fare.

As Norma set before me a second dish brimming over with sherry trifle, and placed a plate above the dish and slightly to my left, containing some jam sponge, a huge slice, plus some home-made lemon curd tarts, the door to the stairs opened and two more young fellows walked into the already crowded room.

"Hi Boyzie!" they both roared, and both slapped me heartily on the back. "How're you doin', mate?"

Two young soldiers, both home on leave from the army, and both there for just a few more days before going abroad, one to Northern Ireland, the other to Germany to await a possible posting out to Iraq. It was so good to see them both. I had not met either of them for some time, not in fact since 1979, when I had last seen their mother. Now, both were six-footers, and had turned into tall, handsome and very fit young men. Randle was in the Paras and his younger brother, Dominic (Dom) was in the Royal Engineers. Both were currently staying with Norma, and thoroughly enjoying their period of leave, they said. I had not been told they were there, and they had stayed upstairs out of the way until we were all settled down, enjoying our tea, so they could come down and give me a surprise!

"Oh guys! It's so gud to see you again," I said, and the three of us shared a manly embrace, to cheers and shouts from all others present.

Tea at Norma's that day was a most happy and enjoyable occasion. Afterwards, when all the pots were washed etc., etc., Norma's son, Kenny, said:

"Shall we all go down the pub later then?"

That met with a rather mixed reception from the assembly. All the blokes present and most of the women seemed to favour the plan. The grandchildren, however, were not so sold on the idea! Eventually Norma's two youngest daughters, Louise and Julie, said they would stay and look after the children, and also Elaine, Vinny's wife, who was pregnant again, and Ed's wife, who was also expecting another child, said they would both stay, as they had no desire to go out drinking! As for the rest of us, we were all well up for a few drinks down the Swan, so we repaired there in groups.

I went along with Kenny and Sue, Eddie and Vinny, who had become my minders for the afternoon, plus Norma, who held on to my hand as we walked along to the pub

"Ye dawn't mind me holdin' on to yo' do yo', luv?" she asked me.

"No! No Norma, not in the least. Hey! What a fabulous tea. It was really good of you to invite me over, luv. I really do appreciate it."

Norma squeezed my arm in hers and laughed good-naturedly.

"Eeh, hark at 'im! Dawn't he talk luvley?"

The others laughed boisterously.

"Quite the little gentleman ain't he though?" said Vinny.

"A proper Lord Fauntleroy an' aal," rejoined Ed, and there was more boisterous laughter.

I felt very embarrassed. Norma gave her younger sons one of her withering looks.

"Hey! Yo' behave yersel's now, aal reet, lads?" she said, and she meant it too.

"Sorry mate! No offence meant, eh marrer?" the two lads said, and both slapped me warmly on the back.

We went into the pub, and the bar became covered with glasses full of beer, wine etc., as we all bought our drinks or had drinks purchased for us. The party was in full swing, and I was thoroughly enjoying myself!

At around 8.30 p.m., they were putting out the buffet on the bar! There was loads and loads of food, because it was still a public holiday for most people up there. Nobody would be going back to work in the pits, the factories, or even at the local council offices until Monday, 7th January, and everyone was determined to enjoy the long break. At 9.30 p.m. there was bingo, and they played five games. Norma won two of them decisively, and the last one paid out. We all had a good drink on Norma before the end of the evening! The place was literally heaving with people by 11 p.m., and Fred Dingle, my brother-in-law, along with a large contingent of the male members of my sister's clan, arrived at the Swan well before closing time!

"Enjoyin' yersel, mate?" yelled Kenny, one of Norma's sons.

"Aw yeh!" I rejoined, with a big smile on my face, and I was, I really was!

Time passed, and at around 1 a.m., the place started to empty. The landlord had obtained a special licence for the holiday period, so he could stay open and have entertainment, food etc., but in the next few weeks there were to be changes a-plenty at that establishment. New kitchens were being installed, and the Swan was about to make a leap into the twentieth century in a big way, which would be very much appreciated around there and beyond.

It was time there were a few four or five-star pubs, clubs and hotels in that region, and from February onwards, the Swan would certainly be one of those four-star places! That was all in the future. One step at a time, eh Boyzie?

☙❧

I found myself walking home with Norma at around 1.45 a.m. in the morning on 3rd January.

"There's a gret big moon lookin' dahn on we, do' yo' knaw?" said Norma as we walked along towards her house. "I luv the moonlight, dawn't yo', Boyzie?"

I was feeling a little woozy and very well fed. I was also feeling ecstatically happy.

"Aw yeh, aw do!"

"That's gud! Aw like someone who's a bit romantic, like me!" she said, as she squeezed my arm in hers.

I responded by putting my other arm around her, and we walked along like that until we came to the corner of her street.

"Fancy a nightcap when we get in?" she asked in her deep husky voice.

"Aw reckon so!" I agreed, and we walked on towards her house in Lennon Street.

When we got indoors we found that most people had gone up to bed. We shifted the four cats that were still indoors off the sofa and settled ourselves down there, kicking off our shoes.

"Cocoa?" asked Norma.

"Ay, why not?" I agreed, feeling that perhaps I should not indulge in drinking any more alcohol.

"Dawn't yo' move, now! Aw'll be back jus' now, so mek' yersel' comfy, okay?"

"Reet," I said, slipping into the local way of speaking without even realising I had done so!

I stripped down to my underpants and socks, and sprawled out on the couch. Norma was not long, and was soon back in the room with a big jug of hot cocoa and a plate of tarts and ginger biscuits.

"Aw'll put 'em ovver 'ere on the table for now, eh?"

"Ay," I said sleepily.

"Shift ower, then!" she said, as she climbed onto the double put-you-up sofa beside me.

She had stripped down to her bra and panties, and was lying beside me, daring me to put my hands all over her silky body! I felt excited! I felt heady! I wanted her! I wanted her badly!

20

A T 8 a.m. on the morning of 3rd January, I lay on the double put-you-up beside Norma, who was still sleeping. I remembered with pleasure the wonderful love we had made in the early morning hours, and although my head was throbbing that morning, I reckoned the previous night and all it had entailed had been well worth it. I laughed when I thought of her making the big jug of cocoa, which I dare say still stood on the table along with the plate of tarts and ginger biscuits! There would be a cover on that, but even if there wasn't, well, what the hell did it matter?

I felt wonderful, apart from the throbbing in my head, and that would go as soon as I got up and had a glass of water, or something cool to drink. Nobody else had stirred as yet, at least I did not think so anyway. We lay together, wrapped in one another's arms, Norma Townley and me! Whoever would have thought it, me and Sandy Christmas's cousin, Norma? Well, there we were, and that was that, and all about it, as Grannie Annie would have put it! I smiled to myself. I wondered if Grannie Annie would have approved of Norma, given the lifestyle she had followed over the years, still, all that was in the past now.

She stirred.

"Hello Boyzie! Ooh! My head's thumpin' hinny! Wot abaht yours, pet?"

"Yes, same here, an' my mouth feels like a rat died in it!" I confessed.

Norma laughed.

"Wot a night, eh hinny?"

"Ay! Wot a night indeed!" I agreed.

Norma pulled herself up into a sitting position then leaned across and kissed me hard full on the lips.

"Thanks for las' night, pet! Aw reckon yo' are a 'five-star' lover, hinny!"

"Thanks! Can I take that as a recommendation?"

We both laughed, and I too hauled myself up into a sitting position on the couch that had served us well! Norma got up.

"Tea?" she asked as she walked into the kitchen in her bare feet.

"Please luv," I rejoined.

I heard her turn the radio on to BBC Radio Two. It was a news summary:

"And finally… the three young blind men who were attempting to climb Mount Kilimanjaro and raise over £250,000 to help cure river blindness in Africa have achieved their goal! At 5.35 a.m. this morning, our time, Philip Mackie, Graham Roddis and Steven Gregson set their feet upon the summit of Mount Kilimanjaro. They are now waiting for helicopters to airlift them back to their families and friends, who are assembling at their base camp to welcome them on their return. However, we understand that, at present there is a violent blizzard in progress, so they may have to wait some time before being reunited with their loved ones and others who have worked to ensure that they achieved their dual goals. Speaking just a short time ago, their spokesman, Philip Mackie, said they were cock-a-hoop at having achieved their dual aims of reaching the summit and raising so much money towards their desired goal! We wish all the very best, a Happy New Year and a safe homecoming to you lads - all three of you!"

The music began to play! I lay back, a smile covering most of my face! So, they had successfully climbed Mount Kilimanjaro! Well done, lads!

As Norma approached me, holding a mug of hot sweet tea out to me, I made a conscious decision! I was going to turn my life around, and last night had been the beginning. No more wasting time! I would make the most of my talents and my situation. For me, as well as for Andy, for Sue and for Rob McCallasky, also for everyone else alive or deceased who loved me or cared about me, I would make a conscious effort to achieve my goal. By so doing, I knew that eventually, I would attain my earnest wish to reach the top of my own Kilimanjaro!

With that thought uppermost in my mind, I finished my hot sweet tea and got up off the couch. Another day had started, and there was plenty to occupy my mind. I quickly found my clothes, pulled them on and went to the bathroom. I was feeling good. I was feeling positive. I was determined to reach the summit of my own fictitious mountain.

ISBN 142517821-9